A REPUTATION
TO UPHOLD

A REPUTATION TO UPHOLD

BY

VICTORIA PARKER

Published in Great Britain 2013
by Mills & Boon, an imprint of Harlequin (UK) Limited.
Large Print edition 2014
Harlequin (UK) Limited, Eton House,
18-24 Paradise Road, Richmond, Surrey, TW9 1SR

© 2013 Victoria Parker

LP

ISBN: 978 0 263 24010 8

Printed and bound in Great Britain
by CPI Antony Rowe, Chippenham, Wiltshire

For Tony, who has developed a saintly patience with regard to his 'missing' wife. For my amazing children, Ben and Issy, who graciously accept when Mummy is busy. And for Megan Haslam and Kathryn Cheshire for their keen insights and endless encouragement.

Thank you all.

And finally, I dedicate this book to Nanna Beena, Auntie Dot, Lynn, Helen and my beautiful sister, Phillipa. To always remember that life is not about waiting for the storm to pass… it's about learning to dance in the rain. As my characters Dante and Eva are about to discover…

CHAPTER ONE

'DON'T DO THIS to me, Finn. Please. Not today.'

Over the din of society's elite, Eva St George crushed her mobile phone against the shell of her ear and sank a fingertip in the other. Hoping the snowy crackle was a particularly bad line and not an indication that her brother was still knee-deep in Switzerland.

'Damn.' Pushing off the oriental silk-covered wall, she swerved through the cliques—women dripping in jewels, adorned in the latest haute couture, and male powerhouses garbed in bespoke evening wear. And all the while her eyes were locked on the ornate double doors leading from London's most prestigious ballroom. 'Finn, give me a minute.'

Twenty-foot banners hung from the high ceiling in swathes of candyfloss-pink emblazoned with crystal love-hearts—the emblem for Breast Cancer United, the charity Eva and Finn supported.

One night a year, together, they launched the fund-raiser in honour of their mother.

Right now, the omission of togetherness was the sting of a needle sinking into her heart.

Palm flat, she pushed the heavy oak and swept into the vast reception of the Royal Assembly Rooms, wobbling on her five-inch heels as plush fawn carpet gave way to sleek graphite marble.

'Okay. Talk to me. Where are you?'

'Look, sis, I'm really sorry. Every airport is closed. I've even tried to pay some rookie half a mill to fly me there but he can't get clearance.'

Pain exploded behind Eva's eyes and her hand shot up to her temple. 'Oh, God.'

'You can do this, Eva.'

Eyes darting this way and that, she spotted an alcove and slunk into the small space, swallowing past the wretched knot in her throat. 'Finn. They're expecting both of us. How can I possibly…?' She stopped herself short. Inhaled long and deep, then pursed her lips, releasing the warm air in one soft stream. Knowing full well she *could* do it on her own; she just didn't relish the thought. Speaking in front of hundreds of people who were no doubt waiting for the 'Diva' to nosedive wasn't the nicest prospect in the world. Not only that, in a strange sort of way it felt as if they were letting their mother down. And, since her death, Eva had let her down enough. But the last thing she wanted was for Finn to worry or feel guilty.

'Don't worry, okay? I can handle this.'

'Of course you can,' he said with an encouraging bluster that said he wasn't entirely convinced. 'We're talking about the woman who has just won the admiration of Prudence West, the soon-to-be Duchess of Wiltshire. Congrats, by the way.'

Eva rubbed her temple, waiting for her brain to catch on to the change of subject amidst the escalating throb, as she mentally altered a speech for *two* speakers. Problem was, it was taking a while and, by the time she realised what she was doing, her fingers wore more make-up than her face.

Scrambling in her vintage clutch for a tissue before she ruined her best dress, she said, 'Thanks, Finny. Prudence West is lovely. She adored my gown designs.'

'So she should—anyone with an ounce of taste can recognise a star in the making. Westminster Abbey, huh?' His deep voice paused as if he were relishing every word. 'My little sister under the royal spotlight. I'm so proud of you.'

Eva smiled and thought, not for the first time, how much she missed him. Finn was the only sane person in the family. Well, as sane as any jet-setting racing driver could be.

Tissue-hunting abandoned, Eva slipped her fingers from her clutch and leaned against the narrow ochre wall. 'I can see perfectly well what you're doing and I love you for it. And by all means give me an Abbey full of duchesses and I'll collude in the art of dazzling every one. Then sit me behind my machine or in my design studio and I'll make their every dream come true. But when it comes to this...' A heavy sigh gushed from her mouth, making her lips tingle with dryness. 'Dad's here too, playing devil's advocate over his flurry of ex-wives as they hurl daggers at each other. Honestly, Finn, the man would give Henry the Eighth a run for his money. He's half cut, making an utter fool of himself. Why can't he have more respect, especially tonight?'

'Head high, turn a blind eye.'

'Good in theory, lousy in practice.' With her free hand she rubbed her bare shoulder to ward off a sudden ominous chill. 'I've worked so hard for this, Finn. If something goes wrong tonight my face will be splashed on every tabloid in the country.'

'Nothing is going to go wrong. Listen...' she heard him inhale; the fact that her stoic-under-pressure sibling felt the need inched her tension levels as high as the opulent chandelier filling the reception '…I was worried about you. I know how much today means to you. So I sent…'

A group of guests hustled past and she turned her back to them to face a mural of the Angel Gabriel filling the inside wall of the alcove. She just hoped it was a good omen. 'Sent? Sent what?'

'He won't crowd you but he'll be there if you need him.'

Need? She didn't *need* anyone. To be continually let down? No, thanks.

Hold on… *He*? A thread of unease tightened around her chest, then unravelled so fast her heart began to whirl. 'He? Who's he? You keep breaking up.'

'I've…asked Vitale…come in my place.'

Before her eyes the Angel Gabriel morphed into Lucifer, horns and all, while Eva went up in flames. '*Dante*? No way—call him off.'

'Call him *off*?' A dark chuckle hummed down the line. 'Despite his bloodthirsty reputation, he isn't a Rottweiler, Eva.'

'Oh, yes, he is.' Voice feathery, her hormones went on a rampage, tearing through her body, piping her veins with more heat. 'He's…he's a snarling, arrogant brute.'

'Hey, he's a good guy. I'd trust him with my life. He won't let me down.' That was exactly what she was afraid of. 'Dante wouldn't be the global success he is today if he purred like a pussycat. You don't know him, Eva.' She knew enough but she had no intention of telling Finn that. He'd ask why and then she *would* be in trouble.

Air whipped in and out of her lungs. Her breasts threatened to escape from the ruched bands of cerise satin and she pressed the flat of her hand to her stomach, begging the tremulous churn to subside. Except her fingers shook so badly her tummy began to swirl like a washing machine on full spin.

'I thought he was staying in Singapore, setting up his precious department store. Not that the man hasn't got enough of them.' That was another thing Finn was good for—dropping information on Dante Vitale without her having to ask questions. She liked to know when he honoured London with his presence so she could go into hiding. Ridiculous. How old was she? Too old. She thanked heaven Finn was trying to speak again before that line of thought took hold.

'He's back to get…' The line hissed. His voice faded in and out. 'I was speechl…'

'Finn! Are you there?' Oh, God. 'I'm going to kill you, Finn, you hear me? With my bare hands.

I'll never forgive you for this.' A total lie. She'd forgive him anything. But *Dante*? Her nerves were already fraying like torn taffeta.

The line's-gone-dead tone resounded through her head like a death blow and her eyes shuttered. Trust Finn to pour petrol on the blaze without even realising it.

Breathe, Eva, breathe.

Okay. She had two choices. Stand. Or topple off her brand-new stilettos. And wouldn't the vultures love that!

No choice really. Standing tall, spine pin-straight, she sucked in air. *Get a hold of yourself. Remember why you're here.*

Of course she could face the upper echelons of society and make her annual speech. So she didn't have Finn by her side—so what? She was a grown woman who was forging her own way to success. She'd just landed one of the biggest contracts of the decade and she refused to let her inebriated father, his ex-wives or the mighty Dante Vitale witness her fall from grace.

It had taken years to climb from the depths of hell after her mother's funeral. Thankfully, the passage of time had washed the grime from her past. No longer was she faced with another hideous front page photograph every morning while every tacky tabloid in the country savaged her reputation. And she wasn't going back there. Ever. Unless it was to showcase her creations and prove to the world she was more than the daughter of a famous designer and a notorious eighties pop star.

Chin up, shoulders pinned, she sauntered back into the ballroom where the air was awash with cultured tones and the tinkle of feminine flirtation.

Turning a blind eye to her father's attention-seeking wave, she hit the wide mahogany bar and gripped the thick brass rail surrounding it.

Smiling sweetly at the bartender, she ordered her usual. 'Sparkling mineral water, please.'

She could do this.

Definitely.

Then it hit her—a deliciously warm musky scent embracing her body in cashmere and teasing her dormant senses to life. Dizzying need, long forgotten, popped her eardrums to bring his dark, rich, Italian lilt direct to her brain in high definition.

'Being a good girl tonight, are we, Eva?'

Skin erupting with a million pinpricks, her stomach wove a torrid sensual spell. It took every stitch of effort to stand tall, keep her head high and inhale enough oxygen so she didn't pass out.

'It's all in a good cause, Dante,' she said, proud

of her strong, if a little sassy voice—the adage 'fight fire with fire' flaming to mind.

Ungluing her sexy heels, she forced an even sweeter curve upon her lips and turned oh, so languidly to face him. And realised the strength of Hercules couldn't have prepared her.

Air locked at the base of her throat as she collided with eyes the colour of burnt umber, gleaming with intelligent purpose and deeply set in a face that could only be described as pure Italian masculinity. Satin-sheen golden skin, an abundance of thick, glossy saddle-brown hair tumbling over his forehead and flicking over his ears.

Eva fiddled with the strap of her handbag to stop herself from tracing the curve of his gorgeous cynical mouth—a mouth she'd spent half her adolescence yearning to kiss.

There was something almost deadly about his beauty, she thought, as she skimmed the wide set of his shoulders, encased in the finest black evening-wear money could buy, the tuxedo only serving to lend his sophistication a ruthless, savage edge.

Eva licked her suddenly dry lips. 'Well, this is a nice surprise.'

'I doubt it,' he said, his fiercely intent gaze searing over her face.

The man saw too much and the idea that he could see inside her, her heart thumping full pelt, her blood rising to boiling-point, peeved her off. She was over this man—had been for years.

Although, in all fairness, it was perfectly natural to still find his dark magnetism so devastating. Right at this minute she knew every woman in the room had been enticed into a delirious state— staring at the forbidden, wanting past endurance. More fool them because never again would he hold power over her. Where her once vulnerable and innocent heart had been deceived, now she knew the difference between lust and love. And she wanted neither. From Dante or any man.

Picking up her crystal tumbler, she relished the cool condensation against her palm and used it to motion to an old client. 'Look, I'm not sure what Finn told you, but I don't need my hand held to speak to a few friends. I'm a big girl. I suggest you go home to your latest mistress. Business or otherwise.'

Renowned for his stupendous retail mind, his financial wizardry and his ferocious talent in the bedroom, Dante Vitale was a one-night wonder. With the exception of his wife, Natalia, of course. If she remembered correctly, that had been a two-month wonder. Almost as long as her father lasted with one of his fine specimens.

The worst thing was, she'd been so pathetically enraptured with him she would've taken one night. But his taste ran to sultry brown eyes, sleek brunettes with svelte sun-kissed bodies. Pure Italianesque. Little wonder he'd never given Eva a second glance. Until she'd literally thrown herself into his path. And even then…

Her face began to burn as the mortal humiliation came back to her in a torrid rush of heat. 'If you'll excuse me, I need to mingle.' Feet bolting, she managed two steps before a steel arm wrapped around her waist and hauled her back to the bar.

Eva shuddered from top to toe, the melting sensation back with a vengeance as a lock of his shockingly thick hair fell across one eye as he tossed her a 'stay put' look.

He ordered a finger of single malt and pinned her in place with the wide span of his hand, only his thumb and forefinger touching her satin sheath. The tiniest contact enough to send all the heat from her face down to her knickers.

'Don't you think your dress is a little revealing, Eva?' he said with a satiric bite. 'This is a charity fund-raiser, not a nightclub.' He knocked back the shot and carefully lowered the glass to the polished mahogany bar.

'There's nothing wrong with my dress and you know it.' It was nun-like in comparison to what his usual dates wore. 'Why are you here, Dante? I understand what Finn was trying to do. He has no idea what happened. But you...' She shook her head. 'You should've refused. Especially since you can't bear to look at me for more than five seconds.'

As if to deny her accusation, he deigned to look at her—with such cold detachment he might as well have tossed the whisky-coated rocks in her face.

'I'm here because I owe Finn, nothing more. As you've accurately pointed out, I have far more *pleasurable* things to do than babysit a loose cannon. But if you think for one minute I intend to break my word to him, you are sadly mistaken.'

She closed her eyes momentarily. 'People grow, people change.'

'No. They do not.' He leaned a touch closer and she went strangely woozy. 'Especially when they still have the power to stop traffic.'

Only Dante could twist a compliment into an insult with that cynical mouth. His dark eyes flickered down her body and she cursed her penchant for decadent ice cream.

Then he continued in that same thick, dark drawl, 'That was quite a pile-up you caused in Piccadilly Circus. Did you enjoy the world staring at your body?'

Distaste filled her mouth. 'That billboard was a campaign for—'

He waved her off with a dismissive flick and Eva sighed. What was the point of arguing with a man who saw everything in black and white? So she stuck with the facts, praying he'd just walk away. 'Go home, Dante. I don't need a chaperone.'

'Apparently you do,' he said, his caustic gaze dropping to the mineral water she held in a death grip. 'At least you're not plastered.'

She gasped. And to think she'd once thought herself in love with the guy!

'You're locked in the past. You don't know me. I drown in work these days.'

'Really.' One word, brimming with derision, and she wondered if he even knew what she did for a living. He'd been in Singapore for the past year or so, Italy before that, but he'd seen Finn on occasion. Maybe he didn't care enough to ask, but frankly she'd had enough of being dragged through the wringer.

Her mouth shaped for speech, ready to tell him what she'd achieved. All about her stunning new boutique, the new contract for the soon-to-be Duchess she'd fought tooth and nail for—

When suddenly he snorted like a displeased horse. 'And what work would that be, Eva?' Eyes glittering, he traced her décolletage, a look that turned almost cruel—a striking contrast to the velvet now stroking his voice. 'Slipping between the warm sheets of the morning papers…*hot* off the press. Now I'm back in London, what will I wake to find tomorrow? I wonder.'

Eva gritted her teeth and tightened her fingers around her clutch, the temptation to swipe the mocking look off his face far beyond her usual realm of control. Honestly, what was the point of defending herself? He'd made up his mind. It shouldn't hurt so much, it really shouldn't. And the only reason her insides felt as if they were being picked apart was because she wanted him gone.

Chin up, she was determined to stand her ground. This time there would be no regrets.

'Is this the support you promised Finn? To come in here, berate me, when you obviously have no idea what I've been doing for the past few years? Claw at my confidence before I have to go on stage? *Wow*. I'll be sure to tell him what a grand job you did. Now, get your hand off me and disappear into the night. That is your usual parting gift, after all.'

Dante tightened his grip on her warm stomach and felt the muscles clench under his palm, the tiny contractions spiking his pulse so hard his jaw set. It took no more than a second to convince himself he was misreading the pain in Eva's eyes. Then he snatched his hand back and set her free.

A wisp of her sultry scent drifted up his nose as she spun with the grace of a ballerina and sashayed through the clumps of dowdy patrons—a dark pink firework amongst a sea of sickly candy, her position as co-founder of the charity blatant in her choice of colour.

Dante tore his gaze from her sinful behind and ordered another shot of single malt.

Maledizione! He'd handled that *really* well. And she was right. He should've told Finn to find someone else. The crackling atmosphere was like a dark storm brewing in the room, threatening to rain destruction on them all.

Flawless, that was the word people used for her beauty. But it was a lie. Her flaws lay buried deep, hidden under dark lashes, lurking in the wary shadows of her mesmerising mossy-green eyes.

Assuming he'd buried his memories was his first mistake, because he could still feel the damp warmth of her blanched almond skin beneath his lips, the pure tone hinting at an innocent enchantment that was her dangerous allure. The only truth was her curves, which should, quite frankly, be illegal.

Heat, swift and decadently erotic, flooded his veins.

Eva St George. Wild child. Fantasy pin-up for every hot-blooded man.

Raising the glass to his lips, he downed the second finger of Scotch, the warm amber liquid lubricating his throat and inflaming the annoyance swirling in the pit of his stomach. He should *not* have touched her again. But if there was one thing Dante loathed it was a woman turning her back on him. He did the walking. He was in control. Always.

It didn't help that the only time he'd ever lost it was with Eva. No matter how many times he insisted he had merely been comforting her on the night of her mother's funeral, he couldn't escape the fact that sanity had slipped from his grasp. And he'd almost taken her...*Cristo*, on the floor of the pool-house!

And tonight. She must be hurting. *That* was the

pain in her eyes. *That* was why Finn had asked him to come. Because he knew Dante would remember. For all her wild ways, she'd loved her mother and watching her struggle with remembered grief was not a sight he relished. That, he insisted, was because of his loyalty to her brother, his *friend*.

The thought of Finn brought him back down into the ballroom with an almighty thud. He had to forget the past, deliver on his promise to Finn and get the hell out of here. He could be nice. For at least twenty minutes.

Sliding a fifty across the bar, he turned to face the bustling glitterati, taking less than five seconds to find her, courtesy of the dress that smothered her luscious body as if poured with silken oil.

Eva now had a flute of champagne in her long slim fingers and curved those famous do-me-now lips to lure another man. *You don't know me. People change, she says!*

He didn't want to hear it. For the first fifteen years of his life he'd hoped, prayed, pleaded for such *change* from his equally wild mother. So he'd switched off years ago to Finn's ramblings about his precious little sister. Diverting conversation had quickly become an art form. Finn naturally had a soft spot for her and Dante liked the man too much to smash his rose-tinted view.

Shaking his head, he crossed the space between them, the stark light of the bar fading as the crowds parted and he moved deeper into the extravaganza; where butlers in black and white vintage garb enticed the waifs with canapés and tall glasses of pink froth, and the pianist seduced with classical opera which seeped through his skin and eased the tension from his spine. By the time he caught up, Eva sat alone at one of the huge round tables, washed in a soft peach hue courtesy of a thousand tiny crystal tea lights.

Sitting on the deep velvet seat beside her, he pinched the stem of her champagne flute and handed it to a passing waiter before ordering his senses to go on mute. 'Here we are again.'

Her dark blonde head snapped around, the long, luxuriant waves swaying about her bare shoulders. 'Can't you take the hint? I. Am. Fine. You need to. Go. Home.'

Dante leaned back, knowing full well he projected ennui. 'No.'

Her eyes glittered with the first sparks of her temper but he had to give her credit because she banked the fire, no doubt disinclined to cause a scene. 'What are you doing back here anyway? I thought Singapore had captured your full attention.'

'Impossible. Nothing is enough to capture my full attention.'

She leaned her perfect body into the back of the chair and crossed her arms, the action slow, controlled, pushing her breasts upward, affording him a delicious view of her satiny cleavage. He allowed his eyes to drop. That was what she wanted, wasn't it? His full undivided attention. It wouldn't last—it never did.

'How stupid of me to forget,' she said, her husky voice mocking. 'Guess I thought business was different.'

Dante tore his eyes from her. 'Singapore was a huge success. Two Vitale department stores in twelve months *and* one of the most lavish malls in the world.'

'You sound disappointed. That wasn't enough?'

'It's never enough.' Now he had his sights set on the biggest prize of all. The jewel in the Vitale crown would be the Knightsbridge store he'd wanted for almost a decade. He just needed to convince the seller that Dante was the superlative choice. Problem was, Yakatani, the staunch Japanese businessman, wanted a family man and that particular vessel had sailed four years ago. Flying the flag of treacherous betrayal.

A swell of rabid emotion, black and cold, inflated his chest and he fisted his hand where it lay on the pristine white tablecloth. When he caught Eva glancing down he stretched his fingers wide.

'So what now?' she asked, a small furrow lining her brow. 'Why come to London?'

'Why not?' he said with a careless shrug that tore at his stiff muscles as he tamped down on the dark current of unwanted, loathsome feeling.

'There's more to it than that. I can see it in your face.'

She saw far too much.

Dante cleared his throat and glanced around the room, content that she would drop the conversation when he wasn't forthcoming. Seconds blurred into minutes of warding off the waves of sensuality that poured effortlessly from the woman beside him, which only served to heighten his determination in what now felt like an enjoyable exercise in self-restraint.

So he focused on the towering glass vase taking centre stage on the table, overflowing with cream and dusky pink blooms, each rose delicately wrapped in ivory voile to cup the open bud, and streams of pearls cascading from a lofty hydrangea to pool upon the tablecloth. And, before he knew it, his mind's eye trailed those very pearls over every inch of Eva's body, skimming up those long satiny legs and teasing them between her thighs, where she was hot and wet—

Cristo, for the life of him he could not understand why fatal attraction still poured through his blood…scoring his cheekbones. For a second he wondered if he'd made a sound.

'Dante, are you okay?'

There, he had his answer, Dante noted, without allowing himself to react.

Lazily, he shifted in his seat. Turned and raised one dark brow. '*Sì*. Of course.'

'Well, you didn't answer me,' she said. And for a second he was thrown, his back nudging the velvet pad of the chair. When was the last time someone had the audacity to demand an answer from him? Then again, this was Eva and he should've expected nothing less. Any woman who could turn sweet grieving vulnerability into an all-out seductive war on mankind took daring to a whole new level.

Dante yanked at the sleeves of his white dress shirt until shards of diamond light bounced off his platinum cufflinks. He didn't suppose Eva would be a risk to his deal. She was more front page scandal than the business section type and he needed to talk about something before he touched her.

'I was considering your question: why London?'

He drew his answer out. Waited until he had her rapt attention. Waited to feel the power of the word on his tongue, the weight of it lifting his spirits. 'One word. Hamptons.'

'Nooo,' she breathed, evidently interested. Although he guessed it was merely the conditioned response of a practised woman.

Still, he allowed himself a small smile. It was almost his. He could feel the power of ownership fizzing in his blood.

'Hamptons have the most beautiful departments I've ever seen,' her voice now wistful.

Dante cottoned on to the reason for her enthusiasm. Shopping. Every woman's idea of nirvana. To someone like Eva, he imagined the experience akin to an orgasm.

With mind-blowing speed and precision, his imagination inflamed, offering him an erotic image of Eva exploding under his fingertips…beneath his mouth…coating his tongue. Her glorious body arching like a bow…

A loud female voice shot through the haze and Dante winced. *Maledizione*, he needed sex—to drive out the tension of the last few weeks that had slowly, surely pervaded his body. That was the issue here. It had nothing to do with *her*.

'Ladies and gentlemen, please give a warm welcome to our co-founder, Eva St George.'

Rapturous applause filled the air and Dante watched the rose hue drain from Eva's cheeks. Watched her throat work, the slender column pulsing.

'Eva? What is it?'

'Nothing. I'm fine,' she said with such ease that he realised his imagination was playing tricks on him. Again.

'Of course you are,' he said as he nodded towards the podium where the operatic beauty who was tonight's entertainment stood waiting. If the card she'd slipped him earlier was anything to go by, she was more than willing to *perform* personally at his request. 'Show them Eva St George, the Princess of the Press.'

She looked at him then. Properly. For the first time since he'd arrived. Her eyes were swirling tempests which spoke of barely concealed anger. Was she still vexed with him? Even after he'd sat and spoken to her for at least ten minutes?

Dante almost asked what more she expected of him, but each guest now stood waiting. Watching.

'You'll be fine,' he said. 'What are you waiting for? Go.'

'It's not that,' she said, scratching at her lower

lip. His eyes narrowed on her short, unpolished fingernails. 'Dante, listen. If I only ever ask this one thing of you, will you do it?'

He didn't like the sound of this. Women and favours were a risky business. There were only three things to be certain of in this life. Ownership, power and control.

'Ask me,' he said.

'Will you leave? Now. Please.'

Eva stepped down from the podium, willing her ribbon-like legs to keep her upright. She'd never thought it was physically possible to want to cry and whoop at the same time but now she knew. All she'd had to do was stand on a stage—in front of *hundreds* of people—on her *own*, and pour her heart out.

But she'd done it. She'd actually done it!

Slightly deaf from a thundering show of hands, she gripped the hand rail and tottered down the steps from the stage. From the corner of her eye, she saw her father beckoning and the temptation to go to him was so strong her feet altered course. But the sight of Claire, wife number six, tugging on his arm stopped her mid-step and she feigned ignorance. There was a happy bubble floating in her chest and no way was that woman popping it.

After a few obligatory handshakes, Eva spotted the heavy gold brocade curtains shrouding the double doors leading onto the terrace. She'd prefer a hot bath and eight hours' sleep, but in her position leaving early was out of the question. So she'd take ten minutes' peace instead. Escape beckoned and, like a prowling cat, she edged around the room, slinking around the guests. She slithered through the small gap in the curtains onto the terrace beyond and quietly closed the door behind her....

And walked into a dense wall of nipping icy air. The fight left her body in one long rush and her shoulders slumped. 'It's over.' Done. For the girl who'd always found large crowds intimidating, she wished her mother could've seen her standing tall.

Wrapping her hands around her upper arms to ward off the chill, she tipped her head skyward, gazing at the beauty of nature's palette—the richest blue imaginable, sparkling with diamanté-studded brilliance. Focused on the biggest, the brightest star and revivified the words she spoke every year, only on this night. *'I miss you. I've made mistakes—so many mistakes—but I'm trying to move on. Make something of my life. Be the person you knew I could be. And I swear I'll make you proud if it's the last thing I do.'*

Closing her eyes, she became lost in time, remembering the sight of her mother teaching her how to work with her nimble fingers. How to stitch another beautifully perfect pearl on dense shot silk and create someone's dream, fill it with romance and beauty and love—all the things she would never have. Only gift. Just as her mother had for women the world over. Until the dark shadows had come knocking and the world went black, everyone left.

Dante.

Thank God he'd left earlier. The thought of him watching her. His beautiful, intense gaze was like a brain-wiping device—

'Eva.'

She flinched and spun around as her hand flew up to her chest to stop her heart bursting through her skin.

'Dante,' she breathed. 'I thought you'd gone. I asked you to.'

He stood in the shadows, face dark, body rigid, his hands stuffed deep in his trouser pockets. 'I gave my word to Finn. Let us call it a compromise.'

'So you sat out here the entire time?'

'Like I said, I promised Finn I would be here if you needed me.'

I needed you once. You left.

As if the last five years had disappeared, the same thoughts began to run through her head, the pictures replaying like an old black and white movie. *Hold me. Touch me. Take me.*

'I don't need anyone.' Not any more. Her warm breath filled the air like a puffy cloud but her voice, icy and brittle, didn't sound as if it belonged to her.

No words. He simply looked out towards the gardens where the cool mist lay like a thick veil, swirling as if beckoning its master back into the Cimmerian lair. And that air of danger seemed to thicken further still, become seductive in its intensity as Dante turned back and closed the short distance between them. Through the dim light she couldn't make out his expression but the heat pouring from his body wreaked chaos on her senses.

'It was a good speech, Eva,' he said, his deep voice imbued with warm sincerity—a hint of the man she once knew. *No, Eva, that man did not exist.* 'Your mother would be proud of you.'

Oh, God. Hold it together. Hold it together. 'Thank you,' she said, but it was a choked sound that tore from her soul and if he didn't leave right now, she was going to…

He growled, long and low, as if he understood, and hauled her into his arms. And the past crashed into the present with heart-stopping brutality.

No thought, no hesitation, she buried her face in Dante's neck, drank in his expensive, darkly sensual cologne and luxuriated in the lashing strength of his arms around her, his long fingers fanning the bare skin on her back…yet he said nothing. He was just *there*. Where she needed him.

No. No! She didn't need him. She didn't need any man. Never had, never would. They let you down, left. Brought nothing but heartache and pain.

So pull away—you have to pull away.

Except…where once cold, she could now feel Dante's hot breath caressing the underside of her ear, whispering over the highly sensitised skin of her neck and she trembled from tip to toe. *Pull away, Eva—do it now.* So why did she ignore the screaming in her head and answer the flaming shrill in her blood to sink her fingers into his gorgeous thick hair and pull him closer still?

Another husky, cursing groan rumbled up his hard chest, vibrating over her aching breasts, and her heart began to thrash against her ribcage. This was not good. It felt good but it was a bad, bad idea. He hated her, for Chrissakes. And hadn't she already learned her lesson with this man?

Loosening her grip on his neck, she eased down from her tippy toes, her fingertips scoring down his sculpted shoulders, unfurling to push him away.

But when her palms smoothed over red-hot silk and she felt the carved perfection of his body, heat splashed through her midriff, flooding her core, banishing all thought and she wanted… *More.*

Suddenly his lips were *there*, hovering over hers, and *oh*, the temptation to touch again, taste him, to see if he was just as thrillingly wonderful as she remembered, made her slide her lips across his in a gossamer-soft stroke…press a moist kiss to the corner of his full mouth…

Dante's entire body hardened to iron ore.…

A flare of electricity danced across her skin and, right then, she knew her mistake. His power had undergone a seismic shift and increased tenfold over the years. Which made him even more dangerous than she'd ever thought possible.

As if he heard her question the force of his dominance, his large hands curved around her waist and cinched vice-tight until she could barely breathe. Then he lifted her entire weight from the floor as if she weighed nothing more than a spool of French lace.

Crushing her body to his, he murmured in her ear, so dark, so quiet, she almost didn't hear him. 'You cannot help yourself, can you, Eva? What is it you want this time? Another night—or shall I just take you up against the wall?'

What? Oh, oh, God. Hot and sharp, a prick of hateful regret stabbed her throat. So when her words came they were laden with biting precision. 'In your dreams, Dante.'

A loud throat-clearing from behind acted like a fist striking glass, shattering the moment. As soon as Dante slackened his grip she jolted back and slammed into the wall, wincing as rough stone bit into her skin.

Claire and her father stood at the top of the stone steps, just watching like a couple of bloody voyeurs.

'Well, well, well,' said Claire. 'What have we here?'

Eva stabbed her palms with blunt nails. 'Oh, I...' What on earth was she supposed to say?

She risked a look at Dante. He stood like cast bronze. Just staring at Eva. Eyes hard, jaw so stiff she fancied his teeth ached. He was angry. No. He was furious. With her. Well, he wasn't the only one!

'I was just saying to Nick, here,' Claire said, all innocence and light, catching Eva's attention, 'where has that *gorgeous* boy got to? I want to be the first to congratulate him.'

Eva felt Dante stiffen beside her and the air became so heavy she could feel it bearing down upon her shoulders.

Ohhh, something was not right. Anguish unravelled behind her breast and Eva knew in an instant that she was about to be very stupid. She was about to fall in the trap Claire was spinning for her. But she was missing something here and she didn't like it one bit.

'Congratulate him?' Eva asked.

Claire's ice-blue eyes glittered with venom. 'Didn't you know? Dante here is engaged to my old school chum, Rebecca Stanford.'

Eva blinked, sure she mustn't have heard correctly. He was getting married again? '*What*?'

'Yes,' said Claire. 'She came to see me yesterday after she flew in from Singapore.'

Eva sucked in air so quickly she almost lost her balance. This was *not* happening. But Claire hadn't finished hammering the nails in her coffin yet.

'We had a lovely lunch with Prudence West. I believe you're designing her gown. Such an honour.'

Eva felt Dante's gaze burning into her cheek. She couldn't look at him. She hated him right now. Years of hard work, clawing her reputation back from the brink. Working eighteen hour days to build the Eva St George brand. And then one look at this devil incarnate and everything was tossed to hell!

'I hope she forgives you, Eva. It's not nice to poach someone else's fiancé.'

Eva reached out for Claire's arm, knowing the violent quiver of her hand betrayed her inner state but she was too far gone to care. 'Listen, Claire, you're taking this all the wrong way. Dante is my...' What? *Friend*? Claire was too clever to fall for that blazing lie. And how much, if anything, had she heard? Brain reeling, Eva tried to think of their last words. Something about...*oh, God*—taking her against the wall! 'There is *nothing* going on here.'

'Didn't look that way to me. Oh, don't worry, my lips are sealed. Although I feel I should warn you.'

From the corner of her eye, Eva saw Dante shift his attention to the swell of her chest. Heard him groan in disgust.

But, before she had the chance to follow his gaze, Claire spoke. 'You haven't taken the microphone off your dress.'

CHAPTER TWO

DANTE'S HAND SHOT to the ruffled bodice of Eva's gown and he curled his fingers around the small black mike, warm from her—or should he say *their*—body heat and tore it free.

He dropped the plastic shell to the frosted stone and crushed it beneath his heel in a satisfying crack.

'Please tell me...' she whispered, standing tall, lifting her chin in the face of adversity '...that what just happened didn't really happen. I'm just in some nightmare. I mean, *you* are here, after all.'

Dante held up one flat palm to prevent another word until he'd at least shaved the edge off his volatile mood and figured out what the hell was going on.

Nick St George paused as his viper wife tried to tug him back into the ballroom and Dante fired the spineless man with the Vitale glare before they disappeared from view. How could he have stood there and let that bitch set Eva up for a fall? What she was hurtling into he had no idea, but he was determined to find out.

As for him…*Cristo*, he'd bet his Lamborghini that within five minutes Rebecca would hear of his *apparent* indiscretion. A shaft of unease fired through his gut, yet, as quickly as it flared, he thrust it away. Rebecca would be easily placated. The good old-fashioned way.

Eva smoothed her tight sheath over her curvaceous hips, brushing the wrinkles free. 'I have to get out of here,' she said. 'I have to think.' Head swiveling, she searched the floor. 'There's little point going back in there; Claire will have me hung, drawn and quartered by now.' She spotted her bag leaning against the old stone wall and bent over to snatch it up.

Dante's heart rate kicked up a few thousand beats per minute as the heart-shaped curve of her full derrière filled his vision and brought forth a multitude of sinful images.

Cristo, she was lethal.

He tore his eyes away as she straightened up and shimmied past him, heading for the stone steps. 'Well done, Dante; you've most likely just ruined me. At the ball in honour of my mother!'

Dante blinked. '*I* have ruined *you*? Forty minutes I've been in your company and already you have wreaked havoc in my life.' Every time. *Dannazione*, the woman never failed.

Pausing on the edge of the top step, she swung around, mouth agape. 'What exactly have I done to you? Just tell Rebecca Stanford the truth. I was… upset. You came for Finn and you gave me a…a… brotherly hug.'

Brotherly? He still had an erection that minus two degrees couldn't diminish. There was nothing fraternal about that!

'Siblings do not kiss each other,' he bit out.

He wished the lighting were better so he could see if the flush on her chest was real. Because he was sure the woman had just propositioned him. Again. She was no innocent. She knew where kisses led. Given another three minutes, he could have taken her up against the bloody wall.

Cristo, she was like a Venus flytrap. Luring, bewitching, with that sweet, grieving vulnerability, which she knew would beguile him. Because, in a once-in-a-lifetime moment of weakness—so she'd known she was not alone—he'd told her the brief details of burying his own mother. For two minutes of time he'd resurrected the fetid blend of conflicting emotions, only to bury them back into the depths. So the siren knew *exactly* how to play him.

'Well,' she said, 'obviously, I was of unsound mind. Because I have no interest in you. *Whatsoever.* In fact, you can rest assured hell will freeze over before I touch you again. Give me some credit, for heaven's sake, I've got some pride.'

Something close to affront clawed down his chest. It was as unsettling as it was idiotic.

'Just tell Rebecca you hate me,' she went on. 'Nothing but the truth. I promise you within seconds your stunning fiancée will tumble back onto your well-frequented bed!'

Dante almost laughed. Almost. 'My sleeping arrangements seem to bother you, Eva.'

Her head reared. 'Hardly. I couldn't care less what you do. But you could've told me you were getting married,' she said, her husky voice fracturing with a heartfelt anguish that made him pause mid-step, frowning at the contradiction between her words and tone. 'I was caught completely unawares. I could've at least come up with a better look than a shocked guppy for a retort.'

'Because appearances are everything, of course.' There was truth in that sarcastic inflexion and he knew it. She knew it. Any bad press would smash his deal to kingdom come if he didn't play it carefully. And, as for Eva…

Clip clopping down the steep stone slabs in those

ridiculously high, sexy-as-hell stilettos, she continued to chatter incessantly. 'And now they'll all think the worst. That you...and I...' A husky groan poured from her mouth to wrap around his self-restraint and choke it near to death. 'That I'm a fiancée-poacher. A marriage-wrecker! Not the best marketing ploy, wouldn't you agree, Dante?'

'Which is why we need to talk,' he ground out. How could he take control of the situation if he didn't know what was at stake? His brain was still having problems processing what his ears told him. 'Is what Claire said correct? You make wedding gowns and you won the contract for the next Duchess?'

Screeching to a halt on the lower patio, she stood stock-still...then turned around eerily slowly, bristled and nigh on exploded in front of him, arms thrusting in the air. 'Why are you so incredulous?'

Why, indeed?

'Maybe I pictured you drinking yourself into oblivion and sleeping till noon. Partying yourself onto the front pages every day can be exhausting, so they say.' He gave her an unaffected shrug that tore at his spleen. Because suddenly his memories veered from Eva splashed across the headlines to his mother. Stumbling through the door half-dressed. Slurring her words. Polluting the air with the stench of whisky and vomit. Invariably with another man in tow.

'In all honesty,' he continued, the unwelcome memories making his stomach revolt, his voice bitter, 'I never thought you could manage a day's work in your life. So I am surprised. That is all.' Surprised? She might as well have stunned him with a laser gun. He did not like the feeling. It blasted his equilibrium to pieces.

Blinking, her stunned mouth worked around words. 'Oh, just *go away*, Dante, and leave me be. Go seduce your bride. I hope you'll both be very happy. Burning in hell.'

Then off she went, swerving around the cobbled stone path. Dante rocked on his heels, tempted to let her go. The more time he spent with her, the more frustration clawed his insides. She was the most disobedient, agitating woman he'd ever met. So why was he still standing here allowing the frost to travel up his limbs?

'Bloody woman.' With a growl, he caught up with her as she strutted beneath the ornate lamps illuminating the gardens, and the dim glow casting her body with a warm sheen.

Thought vanished. His guts pinched with a peculiar nip. '*Cristo*,' he burst out, making her pause mid-step. 'Your back!'

Unthinking, he reached out, dusting his fingertips across the raw, scraped flesh marring her beautiful almond skin…felt a shudder ripple down her vertebrae before she jerked away.

'Don't touch me.'

Dante set his jaw—she hadn't said that ten minutes ago. Or five years ago. But he was not going *there*. 'Your skin needs treating, Eva.'

She swirled around, scepticism widening her eyes. 'What do you care? If you didn't hear me the first time, I'll tell you again. I'm a big girl. I can look after myself.'

She was right. She didn't need his help. Eva St George, the Princess of the Press, knew exactly how to play the game. And let's not forget, she'd just stood in front of hundreds of people and made a speech from her very soul about the mother she'd adored. That kind of emotional strength was not indicative of weakness.

'Go home, Dante.' Chin up, Eva thrust her shoulders back with a lofty flounce. 'You're fired!'

A humourless laugh burst from his lips. '*Fired*?'

'Your job as brotherly stand-in is over. Quite frankly, you've been appalling. I hope I never lay eyes on you again.'

Fury bubbled in his blood. Why, he had no idea, because technically she was doing him a favour.

Dante stepped forward, close enough to make out the tiny freckles kissing her pert nose, and murmured, 'That makes two of us, *tesoro*.' And he meant it. The woman reminded him of cyanide. Troublesome. Deadly potent. She'd been toxic enough years ago and her seductive allure had somehow quadrupled with age.

'Good,' she said, stepping backward straight onto a patch of black ice.

Dante snatched at her arms, cupping her elbows to stem her fall.

Time stilled as he trailed his gaze over her exquisite face and, the chilly eve forgotten, he pictured laying her down on a bed of grass—the same lush colour as her eyes—curving his hands around her stunning body, feeling the weight of her heavy breasts in his palms, glorying in the sweet sinful taste of her skin. He wanted to cup her face. Take her breath away with his lips. He wanted to kiss her. Properly. No. He wanted to devour that impertinent mouth.

Dante swore he could hear her thunderous heartbeat echo his own. And he knew. Her entire body thrummed with a craving so intense she vibrated with the power of it. She had just lied to him outright. Of course she had. She still wanted him. More than ever.

His mouth twisted, even as he acknowledged the revelation. It was still there. Incomparable. Extraordinary. A ferocious desire that crackled the air with tiny fireworks and wreaked havoc on the exploding senses. His own control was barely leashed, his brain a fog…until she tore from his hold. 'Get your hands off me!'

Dante's jaw went slack. *Cristo*, the way she wielded her sexual power would render a lesser man witless.

'Next time you want to play games, *cara*, I suggest you choose a man unaware of your technique. Despite my reputation, I am extremely particular when it comes to the women I take to my bed. And the hot and cold routine turns me off.'

Her lips parted with a stunned smack and for one second he thought she was going to hit him. And the bizarre thing was, he wished she would.

'I wouldn't sleep with you if the future of civilisation depended on it,' she hurled back before she swivelled on her heel.

A noxious blend of rage, frustration and unadulterated desire swirled behind his ribs. 'Eva, I'm not done with you. Do *not* walk away from me.'

She didn't walk. She marched. He refused to bend to her will and go after her. He was in control. Always.

So instead he watched thick clumps of vaporous air swell in front of his face long after she'd disappeared from view. And, as the anger waned, unease flooded his psyche as he asked himself the very same question he'd asked Eva hours earlier… *What will I wake to find tomorrow? I wonder.*

Slivers of daylight shone through the slits of her duck-egg curtains and, with one last look at the Sunday morning headlines, Eva tugged the top edge of her quilt and watched the mountain of newspaper scatter upon the parquet floor. Pulling the blankets up over her head, she nestled further into the lavender-scented warmth and closed her eyes, trying to block out the bold script etched on her brain like the tombstone of what remained of her career.

Soon-To-Be Duchess Threatens to Give St George the Royal Snip.

Is Diva up to Her Old Tricks?

Watch Out, Brides! Eva's on the Prowl.

'Thank you, Dante Vitale.' Writhing against the sheets, she kicked the blankets away from her over-warm skin, half-tempted to sue him for disclosure.

Then again, what on earth was she thinking kissing him in the first place? You would think the humiliation of five years ago had been enough to last her a lifetime. The only saving grace was that Dante's scathing one-liner about taking her up against the wall didn't appear in print!

Her pride was an ultra-fine thread stretched so taut it threatened to snap at any second.

'Enough.' She was quickly forgetting her new life motto: no regrets. Move on. It was time for a plan. A strategy.

Glancing over at the clock, she groaned when she saw that the small hand had only turned a quarter since the last time she'd looked. Eight forty-five a.m. Still too early.

She needed to call Prudence West. The serene soon-to-be Duchess had left a disarmingly polite message on Eva's answering machine last night before she'd even arrived home.

'Thank you, Claire.'

By then it had been too late to call her back and Eva knew what was coming—'You're fired', delivered with dignified, heart-cracking finality. After all, she knew how destructive bad press could be. She could hardly blame the woman, especially in her position.

The lump swelling in her chest made it hard to breathe. How many more clients would she lose? How could she ensure that business kept walking through the door? This wasn't anything like when she'd started out on her own. This time she had other staff to think about. Her seamstress, Katie, who had two little boys to feed at home. Her assistant, who would have a nervous breakdown if she couldn't go clubbing on Friday night. Not forgetting the rent for her boutique downstairs, which was colossal.

Responsibility tore her insides to shreds. What if she could persuade Prudence West to stick by her? Surely, everyone would follow suit. If she appealed to her, told her the truth…

The buzzer shrilled through her apartment for the hundredth time since seven a.m. and Eva yanked the blankets back over her head. 'Go away!' This was just like when her mother died.

Princess of the Press, Dante had called her. Four tiny words with the power to crush. Because, in all honesty, she felt ruled…almost owned by them. Blood-sucking creatures to whom decency was a foreign concept. This morning they didn't want the truth; they wanted sensationalism. In the past, how many times had she tried to give her version of events, only for her words to be twisted beyond recognition, ensuring she was as red and fiendish as the she-devil herself?

The phone shrilled, making her temples throb,

and she waited until the answering machine kicked in.

'Eva, pick up the phone.' Dante's fierce bark filled the air of her apartment.

'Oh, *great*.'

'I am outside parked at the kerb, surrounded by reporters and I'm warning you, if you don't pick up—'

Thrusting back the covers, she scrambled across the wide dark wood sleigh bed to retrieve her cordless from the bed-stand. Determined to be calm, composed and totally in control.

'*What*?' she snapped. 'What will you do, Dante? Haven't you done enough damage?'

'*Me*?' he said, incredulity and exasperation lacing his voice. 'May I remind you that your reputation precedes you? And do not speak to me of damage when I have just endured thirty minutes of female temper tantrums from my *ex*-fiancée!'

'Ex-fiancée?' she repeated, her mood lifting. And in that moment Eva knew she was a horrible, horrible person. The man undoubtedly brought out the worst in her. But why shouldn't he at least feel a smidgeon of the turmoil she was in?

A long sigh poured from her lips. 'For heaven's sake, just tell the woman you love her.' Where was the man's famed intelligence? No wonder his marriage hadn't lasted long.

A stunned silence, then, '*Love*? What has love got to do with it?'

'Ah, well, say no more,' she said sardonically. 'It's usually why people get married, didn't you know?'

'In your world, maybe,' he growled down the line. 'Let me up, Eva, we need to talk. There's only one way out of this mess.'

'I don't want you here. It'll make things look worse.'

'Believe me,' he said. 'Things could not *possibly* get any worse.'

Oh, yes, they could—he could come up here and she could murder him for the unforgivable things he'd said to her last night. He could witness sleep-deprived Eva, eyes heavy with fatigue. But, more importantly, 'I refuse to provide the wolf pack with even more fodder.' And how could she approach Prudence then? *Oh, it's okay, he always calls for a friendly brunch early on a Sunday morning?* Yeah, right.

She heard him exhale and swore she could feel his warm breath trickle over her collarbone. Reaching up, she stroked the goose-pimples dotting her skin...and then yanked her hand away. What was wrong with her? How could she still crave the man's touch? A man so cynical. So savagely brutal.

'I have the answer to everything,' Dante said in a shiver-inducing low tone. A rich velvet she'd never heard before, didn't trust. It was luring, almost spellbinding.

'You do?' she asked, drawn in against volition.

'*Sì*,' he said, silky as sin. 'The perfect plan.'

'What, like a miracle?' And hold on a minute, why did he want to help her all of a sudden? Yesterday she'd been an alcoholic tramp. Goodness and hearts didn't generally figure in the Vitale phrase book. 'Did Finn send you?'

'No, I have not spoken to him since yesterday. The lines are down. It's either me or nothing.'

Lips parting, she almost told him *nothing* sounded wonderful but something stopped her. The business. Katie's two little boys. The rent.

She thrust her hands through her hair, tugged at the roots, tried to shake out the kinks.

If Dante could help with the press in some way, maybe she should hear him out. The man wore power as comfortably as other people wore shoes and thinking of herself was selfish, right? In reality, she had nothing left to lose.

Dipping her chin, she glanced down and winced

at the cosy, ratty PJs. Hardly the uber-chic designer look.

Drat. There was that pride again.

'Okay. Give me five minutes.'

'Three,' he said before disconnecting.

Mouth agape, she stared at the phone…realised she was wasting valuable dressing time and tossed it across the pearly-pink throw. 'Odious, obnoxious, offensive snake. I must be mad.'

Gripping the thick knot of his dove-grey tie, Dante pushed the silk further up his throat and straightened the lapel of his black jacket. Tension pumped through his blood, making him hard all over—energised, taut, inordinately satisfied he'd given the press the perfect picture of ruthless determination by upending every last one of them from Eva's doorstep.

In one respect he questioned why she hadn't given them the boot herself but on the other hand he was grateful she hadn't unleashed her tongue. He had plans for Miss St George and the sooner he brought her round to his way of thinking the better. Obstinate to the nth degree, he knew he'd have a fight on his hands but the predator in him could already smell the scent of glory.

And why the hell was she taking her own sweet time opening the door?

A seed of a sinister thought detonated and a strange emotion settled in the pit of his stomach, curdling thick and black. Did she have someone in there? In her bed. Entertaining. Was that why she was ignoring the press?

Dannazione, he'd never thought of that. And for the man who was renowned for meticulous planning, that should've told him something. Yes, he assured himself, it told him his deal was hanging in the balance and if she…

Sweat bubbled on his nape and trickled down his spine at the thought of walking in there. Seeing another man in her bed. Her full do-me lips meshed with his.

Heart twisting, it tore from his chest and dropped into the well of his stomach.

The sound of metal sliding across metal filtered from inside and scored his suddenly sensitized skin like talons down a chalkboard.

Rolling his shoulders, he inhaled slow and deep. Yet when the solid oak door swung open he realised the intense lung workout had been an utter waste of energy resources.

There she was. Tousled. With that adorable sleepy look about her. The one he remembered from sleeping over at Finn's and watching an eighteen-year-old Eva tumble down the stairs on legs so long it had taken her an age to fathom the art of walking gracefully. It would've just turned noon and she'd mooch round the kitchen wearing huge earphones and skimpy cotton pyjamas, the small, tight shorts leaving nothing to the imagination.

For a moment he wondered what she wore to bed these days and then cursed inwardly as his blood pressure spiked through the roof.

So he focused on the now. This Eva. Twenty-seven years old and more beautiful than ever. All that gorgeous hair falling down around her face and caressing her bare shoulders. A tiny vest-top in a soft blush colour that threw her dense cleavage into stunning effect and a long dark pink skirt that reminded him of a gypsy. But *Cristo*, it was the bare feet that really snagged him. Perfect little toes painted pearly-white as if she walked on heavenly clouds. And there it was again. That hint of innocence he *knew* to be fake.

'Are you entertaining in your bed?' he asked, his voice so hard it almost cracked his skull. And, just to make sure there was no misunderstanding, he rephrased. 'Are you sleeping with anyone at all?'

'Did you really just say that?'

'Yes.' After all, it would ruin all his plans if she

had a multitude of boyfriends all over the place. Was her rock star still on the scene? A man with a perpetual hangover. The perfect couple.

Dante ground his back teeth. 'Just answer my question, Eva.'

His don't-mess-with-me tone was met with an arch of her delicate blonde brows.

'Good morning to you too,' she said, hand braced on the door frame as if she was half-tempted to slam it in his face. 'You're in a lovely mood this morning.'

He smiled. It was an evil twist, he knew it. 'I'll be in an even better mood when you answer me.'

Firing darts of ire, her eyes drifted to the wall above the door frame, breasts rising and falling as she grappled for control. 'No. I don't... I haven't...' Chin down, she straightened to her full impressive height. 'What exactly does my private life have to do with you, anyway?'

'Plenty, considering the newspapers this morning,' he said, striding past her, not entirely convinced by her claims to single status but willing to give her the benefit of the doubt. For now. 'Haven't you heard? We're the new golden couple.'

She laughed—a hollow sound that serrated his spine. 'There's nothing golden about *you*. Anyway, I haven't managed to get past the front page yet.'

'Then I assure you, you're in for a real treat.'

Dante heard the door click shut and her mocking remark, 'Come in, why don't you,' as he strode down the narrow hallway and found himself in a… cosy lounge flooded with light.

Cream muslin hung in swathes at the wide windows, softening the stark glare of December and bleaching the dark oak floors. Huge, squashy gold sofas—the curling up with a book type—framed a large coffee table and took centre stage around a black Edwardian fireplace. Frames in every shape and size covered the hessian-covered walls—large gilt mirrors and reprints of times gone by—brides of every era and the accompanying fashions. There wasn't a moneyed feel at all. It was tastefully eclectic with a subtle romantic ambience. But, *maledizione*, the clutter sent ants crawling across the back of his neck as if marching down a vine.

'You are still messy,' he said. It used to drive Finn insane. Between Eva and her mother, their family home had been a constant artistic chaos. It was a sure bet you'd be pricked by a sadistic pin or three from sitting on a perfectly innocent-looking chair.

'So shoot me.'

Reluctantly his mouth curved at the petulance in her voice, until his eyes fell on a dressmaker's dummy filling one corner of the room with a volu-minous frothy tulle skirt tacked around the waist. Stepping closer, his breath snatched—the retail connoisseur in him enchanted by the sight of del-icate pearls stitched into the weave.

'By hand?' he asked. Knowing it to be impos-sible because it would have taken her—

'Yes, of course. Took me almost a week.'

Every day he was shown a multitude of beautiful clothing, but this... 'It's exquisite. I see you have inherited your mother's eye for detail. Her unmis-takable genius with fabric.'

Even as she stood behind him he could sense frank bewilderment that he'd complimented her work.

Having been subjected to his father's particularly vicious brand of criticism since the day he'd been torn from his mother's graveside, he had no prob-lem with dishing it out. No longer did it make him angry to hear; it only made him strive to be harder, stronger, more powerful than ever before. But the beauty in Eva's raw talent stopped him dead in his tracks for there was not one fault in any stitch or placement of pearl.

'Why didn't you tell me the extent of your suc-cess last night? Your boutique?'

She gave a little huff. 'Oh, come off it, Dante.

You had no interest in my life or anything I had to say.'

He didn't mistake the touch of hurt in her voice and he was man enough to admit he deserved it. One desperate phone call from Finn, one look into those dazzling green eyes and he'd known trouble was coming. Deflecting it, however, hadn't brought out the best in him and in the end it had been a pointless pursuit.

'I had no idea about your work.' Now he wished he hadn't closed his ears to Finn's animated renditions. Without them, he'd been left with one possible avenue.

So this morning he'd ignored every flammable headline and had his investigators expose her business interests. She'd built her small bridal couture company from nothing. *Nothing.* Laser gun time. Stunned would be an understatement. Where was her inheritance—her mother's legacy? Blowing millions of pounds within a few years on the party scene must've been one hell of a joyride. He assumed that when the money had run out she'd had to make a trade of some kind.

At first glance he'd thought Finn would have provided capital but no, she'd done it all herself, through banking loans and hard work. And he felt something he'd never thought he'd feel for her. A measure of respect.

'Now you do,' she said. 'Except do me a favour and lay off the congratulations regarding Prudence. She's already left one message and I shouldn't think the next royal wants an engagement-wrecker to bless her gown.'

The anguish in her voice sliced at his throat. He knew what it is was like to work night and day with recognition continuing to be far from reach. At twenty-three he'd fought for the chance to save the ailing Vitale empire. The battle had been endless until desperation had forced his father to hand him the reins. It had taken Dante almost six months of working 24/7 to operate back into the black. So he knew the determination, the frustration, the rage.

'Won't stop me trying to change her mind, though,' Eva said with a dose of grit that made his mouth tilt. Ah, there it was. The fight.

'So why are the shutters locked downstairs?' he asked.

'Luckily, I only open the last Sunday of every month. I wanted to contact some of my clients before facing the hounds.'

'It is best you do not speak with them until we get our story straight,' he said, hearing his autocratic tone ricochet off the walls.

A small frown creased her brow. 'Our story? There is no story, Dante, only the truth. If that doesn't set me free I'll just have to wait until the furore dies down. There'll always be other jobs.' But she wanted this. Desperately. Oh, she tried to hide it, but the stiff smile she tried on for size visibly cracked her composure.

She wanted it, just as much as he wanted Hamptons. Neither could afford tittle-tattle. Yakatani not only preferred committed family men but he was inordinately disturbed by tabloid fodder. With plenty of multi-billionaires in the running, he had his pick of the auspicious crop.

Dante considered the tartan wingback chair, decided not to take the risk and walked over to the windows to inspect the street below. Decent enough area for a boutique, he supposed. Mayfair or Bond Street would be better.

Rolling his neck, he breathed deeply. Truth time. Explanations he wasn't very good at because as a rule he answered to no one. 'I had an arrangement with Rebecca.'

He allowed her to soak up the admission, wrestle her thoughts into some kind of order. When her words came they were doused with intrigue. 'What kind of arrangement?'

'I needed a fiancée to close the Hamptons business deal.' And with that one strategic purchase he would make Vitale the biggest retail phenomenon in the world. Then his father would have no choice but to acknowledge his first son—his bastard son—as the rightful heir. Finally he would prove to the old man that he was worthy of the Vitale name. That he was no longer a dirty stain on a virtuous thousand-year legacy. That he wasn't tarnished by his mother's bad blood. That he was strong enough to live only for Vitale and nothing, *nothing* would stand in the way of his success.

Fingers delving into his hair, he thrust the memories back into the dark depths. Locked down his emotions with ruthless efficiency.

'I had no intention of marrying the woman,' he said. One stab at the marital state had been enough to inoculate him against the institution for life. 'I only bumped into her a couple of weeks ago in Singapore.' Dante had known Rebecca from Cambridge days. A striking brunette who had a tendency to flirt with him outrageously. But she had chosen the wrong day and the wrong man to play with.

She'd cornered him and while he'd been sorely tempted to take what was on offer that night, to lose himself, drive out the anger, something had stopped him. Despite her overt sexuality, she'd turned him to stone.

While he'd never been the small-talk type, he had listened. To dampen his fury. To forget his father, his half-brother. It soon became apparent she was neck-deep in debt and needed funds— astronomical amounts. She was desperate. And, like a shark smelling bait, Dante's killer instincts had kicked in and within seconds he'd pounced on that weakness and a business arrangement had been born.

'Oh,' Eva said, 'you must want Hamptons very much.' Warm, understanding, her husky voice wrapped around him, taking the edge off the chill that had been pervading his bones for so long.

And, before he knew it, need hit him with the force of a jet, tearing through his body. It took all of his restraint not to walk over there and slide his fingers across her deep silken cleavage, over her décolletage, up the sweet column of her throat. He wanted to sink into that gorgeous thick blonde hair, tilt her head for his kiss and drown in the sinfully erotic taste of her tongue.

Which was inconceivable for so many reasons; his brain refused to wrestle one to the fore. Putting her troublesome tempestuous nature and loose morals to one side, Finn would never forgive him for slaking his lust on his little sister. And this, whatever *this* was, had turned into business and never the twain shall meet.

So he narrowed his focus, his desire, on the only thing that mattered to him. 'I need this deal, Eva. Except now my business relations with the owner are heading for the toilet. Rebecca claimed it is embarrassing enough for me to be seen embracing '*the likes of you*' without her friends believing her a fool in unrequited love.' She'd even hinted that she'd fallen for him and such lies inflamed his gut.

Dante turned from the view, leaned against the sill and caught Eva stuffing some letters under the plush cushion of the sofa before she sat down. The hunch she was hiding something expired as she curled her long legs under her bottom and writhed to find comfort.

How different she seemed in her own surroundings. She looked sumptuous and snuggly and... He shook his head. Appearances meant nothing. *Business, Dante—focus.*

'I assume all her friends thought it was a lovematch?' she asked.

'Her words. Certainly not mine.'

'So what do you plan to do now?'

Crossing his arms over his chest, he locked on his target. To eyes narrowing warily. He responded to that glimpse of suspicion by raising a dark eyebrow. 'I've already done it.'

'Of course you have, Action Man. Care to elaborate?'

He ignored the sarcasm; she'd thank him soon enough. Instead his mind drifted to earlier that morning. When he'd stood in his office listening to Rebecca's histrionics, mouth shaping to quieten her with a lucrative financial bonus. And all the while his eyes kept drifting to the front page headlines. To Eva. And he knew. Even if Rebecca took another cool million and stood by him, Eva would suffer. A good business reputation was something money couldn't buy and, regardless of fault, of the past, they were in this together. Finn had always stuck by him, whatever the storm, and Dante owed him. He could help Eva while ensuring Yakatani remained happy.

There had been moments; *Cristo*, there still were moments of doubt, of reason—telling him not to trust her. Putting her business acumen to one side, he wasn't convinced she would come over as 'wife' material in front of Yakatani. His investigators might have failed to unearth any recent inflammatory stories but that meant nothing when her weekends could be made up of secluded private parties and dangerous liaisons.

Slowly, inexorably, his gaze roamed over her apartment, the blatant romanticism of her career choice. Something didn't make sense. *She* did not make sense.

Dante scrubbed his jawline with the back of his hand. He'd just have to keep an extra-close eye on her. If only to ensure she played by the rules. *His* rules.

The tension in his midsection eased, just a touch. This plan could work. It *had* to work.

They could have it all.

'I've given the press a story that will melt their cynical little hearts,' he said, knowing his tone was sending the temperature in the room into a rapid decline. 'The real thing.'

The frown in her brow deepened, even as she focused on the fireplace. As if she were somewhere else. In thought so deep her expression was almost dream-like in its intensity.

'The real thing?' she asked, her voice as softly decadent as whipped cream.

'*Sì. Love.*' The word was like poison on his tongue, making it swell, his next words sounding thick. 'For surely there is only one reason I could be torn from the bonds of an engagement. The fact that I've fallen madly in love with someone else. I've provided them with a true romantic fairy tale.'

Without looking up, Eva gave a little huff of disbelief and began to scratch at the arm of the sofa, making patterns of what looked like love-hearts. 'And who is the heroine in this fabricated tale?'

Dante smiled. The half smile that never failed to make women weak at the knees and tumble backward onto a satin drenched mattress.

'You are, *tesoro.*'

CHAPTER THREE

EVA'S HEAD SNAPPED up so fast a spasm shot up the side of her neck and exploded in her ear.

'*What*? Are you *crazy*?'

Fairy tales? Her and…*Dante*?

He hitched those broad muscular shoulders, all lazy insolence, and the dark silk lapels of his jacket rippled over the stark white shirt adorning his chest. 'It's perfect,' he said.

Perfect. He was perfect. From his yummy, thick, overlong tousled hair all the way down to his high-sheen voguish shoes. Perfect to look at. Detestable inside. A bit like Christmas cake.

Her mouth worked around words, trying to free her stunned vocal cords. How dare he? How *dare* he!

He, who just stood there. Wielding a half smile that was nothing short of a weapon of mass female destruction sending her body into nuclear meltdown. A smile that said *roll over and take it*.

Then there was that arch of one sleek dark brow.

Expectant. As if waiting for her to thank him. For what, exactly? Digging her a bigger hole to bury herself in?

'Let me get this straight. You've told the press that you've fallen in love with *me*,' she said, jabbing her index finger into her chest before turning it back on him. 'To save *your* business deal?'

'*Sì*. And your deal with the next Duchess.'

His words tore at the tower of her indignation, making it wobble precariously. Would Prudence West be pacified by such a story? She supposed a woman in love, about to marry the man of her dreams, would understand such a predicament.

'But we'd have to feign a relationship,' she said, sounding horrified even to her own ears. 'In public.' She couldn't do it. It would kill her. Bad enough he was in her apartment. Touching things. Sucking the pleasure she'd always gained from her soothing space and replacing it with wretched visual pictures sure to taunt her for days. But what was worse, far worse, was that while she'd been counting down the minutes until he would leave, he'd been planning on staying for the foreseeable future. With her. A woman he abhorred. So really, 'Who would ever believe us?'

'It is done, Eva. Everyone already believes,' he

said, his voice hardening to steel. The self-satisfied look of earlier being replaced by dark irascibility.

Understanding dawned. He actually expected her to jump aboard the Dante freight train to hell. Without so much as a quibble. In effect, she'd require an industrial-strength fire retardant suit!

'You didn't think to ask me first?' she said, her indignation now fully stoked, voice high octane, ready to smash every glass object within a ten-foot radius. She was in control of her own life, dammit! 'You're so…so arrogant.'

He stood to his full six-foot-three, eclipsing the sun and sucking all the air from the room. And Eva held her breath until she nigh on asphyxiated.

'I am taking control of the situation and fixing it. What have you been doing all morning? Lying in bed painting your pearly toes and rewriting your social calendar?'

'Oooh. You just can't resist, can you?'

The devil-may-care shrug he gave her made her angrier still.

Eva sighed, rubbing her temple. When was he going to start taking her seriously? 'If you want me to admit to something then I'll admit to fretting. Fretting my little heart out and thinking of what to do next. But do you blame me? There is nothing wrong with being concerned about my business. It may be small fry compared to your whale of enterprise but it's mine and I've worked hard for it.' Her business was her life. For however long she had. The only joy in a sea of uncertainty. She'd do anything to keep it afloat, but feigning a relationship with Dante was sailing into depths unknown and she wasn't ready to drown just yet.

'If it is so important to you, where is the problem?' he said, now irritated to the point of explosion.

'I don't like the idea,' she said, risking another glance at him, voicing the only argument she could think of without the need to purge her life story. 'It's lying.'

Frank bewilderment widened his beautiful deep umber eyes. 'Funny how naive has never been a word I associate with you. You want to be successful, Eva? You have to play the game. You want to save your career? Get ruthless.'

The only thing ruthless about her was the way she haggled with her suppliers for a measly two per cent and dashed to the supermarket when her favourite ice cream was on special. She preferred to play fair. And she loathed lying. Blame it on the tales she'd heard spouting from her father's tainted lips as her mother lay sick in bed. Blame it on the press for painting her as an alcoholic, drugged up, sexual assassin. Whatever. Lying to the world, to the soon-to-be Duchess, with Dante, made her feel…dirty, somehow.

That must be why she was scratching at her neck. Why her skin felt too tight. It had nothing to do with his presence filling the room with a dark feral aura that made her feel equal parts aroused and scared witless. How could she possibly hide this ridiculous, malapropos attraction when *he* wanted it on full show? For everyone to see…

She gripped the squashy arm of the sofa until her knuckles screamed. 'Whoa, hold on. What's Finn going to think?'

Dante rubbed over his lips with the flat of his hand and Eva fancied she'd just taken a chunk out of his invincible armour.

'I will explain everything and he'll realise that such a story is in our mutual interest. I will *not* risk losing Hamptons and it's clear to me you've worked hard to gain your professional standing. So let us make the most of a bad situation.'

Why was one more department store so important to him? Was he so power-hungry? She understood ambition but, hell's bells, he was one of the richest men on earth. It was said he could turn one dollar into a million within an hour. Sell noodles to a Chinaman, green grass to the Irish.

It was seriously tempting to use that power for her own ends. If she lost custom, she would never meet next month's rent. Her staff would be out of jobs. Life as she knew it, the success she'd fought for, would end.

Could it really work? She was so desperate she wasn't sure she was thinking straight. He made everything sound so simple but simplicity had never figured in her life. There was always a black figure lurking around the corner. Ready to pounce.

'Rebecca will know the truth,' she said as needles of doubt began to pop his plan. 'What's to say she won't pull the plug? Next Sunday she may have sold her story to the papers and we'll be right back to square one.'

The look he tossed her made her feel ten kinds of a fool. 'Ah, *tesoro*, so little faith. Rebecca was the first to know of our affair.'

Never mind thinking on his feet, the man was two steps ahead of time!

'We haven't had time for a love affair,' she said, flinching as the words *love affair* tripped her heart to miss a beat. 'I only clapped eyes on you last night for the first time in years.'

'Precisely. One look and we knew. Rekindled love affairs are the sweetest, so they say.' His voice was jaded silk as he turned away to peruse the flea market knick-knacks on her Edwardian mahogany occasional table.

Rekindled. Right. That made perfect sense. Oh, God. His sharp, cunning intellect sliced her every objection to shreds. But, looking at it another way, he'd clearly thought it through and decided it could work. Still…

'I don't imagine she was very happy.' She'd bet her best sewing machine the woman was neck-deep in love with him. Women with broken hearts could be problematic. Make the most impulsive, illogical decisions…

Digging her blunt nails into her palms, she slammed the brakes on her reminiscences and shifted on the sofa, desperate to stand but knowing she'd only pace and Dante was making her dizzy enough.

Picking up an antique mother-of-pearl trinket box, he ran the thick pad of his thumb over the inlay and she'd swear she could feel that very touch glissade down the sensitive skin beneath her ear and she shivered wildly.

'She was beginning to lose perspective,' he said, voice hard, dark. 'Blending fable with reality. I wanted a business arrangement, not a twenty-four-hour migraine.'

In that moment Eva had no idea what she ever

saw in him. Or why her body craved his touch. He was despicable.

'Obviously the poor woman fell head over her stilettos,' she said, remembering the shattering pain of hurtling into mindless oblivion for this man. 'I almost feel sorry for her.'

'Save your pity,' he said, lowering the small trinket back to the table with a surprisingly gentle touch. 'Women are incapable of love. Unless it comes with a million-pound price tag.'

'Good grief, you're abnormally cynical.' What made a man think in such a demeaning way of women? All women?

'Realistic, *tesoro*.'

'So how come you trust me?'

'I don't,' he said in a casual tone that completely belied the tension radiating off him. 'It is dangerous to place faith in another. Especially when the outcome is of the utmost importance.'

Slumping back into the soft embrace of the sofa, she said, 'Oh, charming.'

'The difference is you have just as much to lose as I. This is not just about money to you.'

Good point. And did it really matter if he trusted her or not? Her heart ached for him to believe in her but, then again, her heart had always been on the stupid side where he was concerned.

Business—she had to focus on business. He was right. This was the only way. On her own it would be hard, maybe impossible to fix such catastrophic damage. They had a far better chance together.

'Okay. What would I have to do?'

A small smile lifted the corner of his mouth. The victorious type. In truth it didn't matter what type it was, it was just as lethal as the rest of him. Also highly premature. She hadn't *technically* agreed to anything.

'Go out,' he began in that silky sinful drawl. 'Attend a few dinners with Yakatani. Play my loving *devoted* fiancée.'

Fairy tales.

Everything stopped. The room morphed into a black and white blur as her vision began to swim as the enormity of his suggestion hit her with the thwack of a hammer-blow to her head.

An unseen hand gripped her heart, the fingers spreading to her throat, squeezing relentlessly until her pulse thudded in a rapid beat. Yet somehow, knowing his fierce shrewd gaze watched her every move, she managed to choke out a laugh. 'Ah, well, there we have our first problem. I don't do devotion.' Nothing but the truth. She didn't want a relationship of any sort—never even *had* a real relationship before.

'Ah, yes,' he said. 'Eva, footloose and fancy-free. Why does that not surprise me?' Dark, savage and wickedly sharp, Dante's tongue was like a blade slicing across the room, lacerating her skin, gashing open another wound. It took every shred of strength she possessed to lift her chin and affect a careless shrug that almost ripped her shoulder blades in two.

It didn't matter to him why she felt so strongly. He was here to save his deal. She was a means to an end. But Eva knew the limitations of her life.

The script had been written years before by one of the most renowned specialists in the world. The moment she'd heard 'high risk' she'd known with bone-deep clarity she would never experience love or the joy of having a family of her own. She couldn't tempt fate. Her mother's death was a living, breathing thing inside her, reminding her of the destruction one woman's demise could cause. Eva refused to take the risk. Refused to expose herself to such pain.

And what exactly was she missing out on anyway? She doubted true love even existed outside the imagination of youthful naivety.

She'd never forget the day her father had left. After her mother had endured another dose of chemo. For twenty years Libby St George had devoted her life to her husband, gave him two children, curbed his alcoholic tendencies and sang like the proverbial groupie at his every concert—whilst building a successful career of her own. And the day his wife needed him more than ever was the day he'd left.

It was Eva who'd picked up the shards of their fragile world. Eva who'd stroked away every tear. Eva who didn't make it to design school that term or the two long, heart-shattering years that followed. Eva who hid every newspaper showing her father on another drunken binge, invariably wrapped around a leggy brunette.

If that were payment for love and devotion—if *that* was true love—such utter heartbreak—she'd rather live her life out completely dependent on herself.

Clearing her throat, she directed her voice to sass. 'Yes, Dante. Footloose and fancy-free. That's me. So, you see, I can't possibly feign a relationship with you. I wouldn't know where to start. And, as for attraction…' A *ppff* vibrated over her lips. There'd be no feigning *that*.

The air shifted, tilting the room on its axis, as he prowled across the room towards her. She felt hunted and it was a dazzling, terrifying experience. Each lithe stride was a thump of her heart and a beat of heat through her blood, until everything melted when he braced one large hand on the sofa arm and the other across the high back, caging her in.

Brooding and fierce, he leaned forward and her brain was attacked by the infusion of his expensive scent. Raw enough to strip away the layers of her anguish.

'Are you saying it is impossible, Eva? To *fake* it.'

'Not impossible,' she said, air stuttering in her lungs as her internal organs went on strike. 'Just a bit of a stretch.' *Push him away, Eva, push him away.*

'Do not lie, *tesoro*, even to yourself. I can hear your heartbeat from the other side of the room.'

Exactly. How mortifying was that?

She stared at his full, dark red lips, unable to move. Her entire body was liquid. A boneless, quivering mass of thrumming desire.

'That would be the clock, Dante. Your welcome in my home is coming to an end.' He had to leave now. Before she did something very, *very* stupid. For the second time in the last twenty-four hours.

His breath trickled over her face, warm and alluring. Spellbinding. He dipped his head and lightly grazed his jaw up her cheek, the friction a delicious firework of sensation. And all the willpower in the world couldn't have prevented the mini explosions in her midriff, the ripples that danced up her body. Piping her veins with heat. Making her breath hitch.

'Ah, Eva, we have enough chemistry to blow up a small country.'

Blinking over and over, she said, 'We do?' *Oh, boy.* Was he saying he felt the same way?

She would laugh if she had the strength to fight through the painful irony. Of all the times she'd wanted him to crave her, only her, he finally desired her when it was too late. 'Explosives are dangerous, Dante.'

'Very dangerous,' he murmured, his deep voice sliding over her, dark and sensuous, like a physical touch.

And then, *oh*, he did touch. His lips shimmied over the soft spot between her neck and shoulder and her lashes fluttered to a close.

'Therefore not to be trifled with,' he went on, before flicking her earlobe with the tip of his nose.

A moan threatened to trip from her lips but she caught it in the nick of time. Determined to stay strong. Not to cry out for more. More pleasure. More pain.

'Eva…' he said, her name another caress, sliding off his tongue with all the practice that had once made her name an endearment. When she was young, stupidly naive, she'd fancied he said it as if she was the most special thing in his world.

The past blended with the present as his heat surrounded her, drawing her in. Without conscious thought, she reached up…touched the smooth satin of his jaw. Satin over steel, his skin smouldered, scorching her fingertips. And Eva—now a moth to a flame—turned her face until they shared one breath. Until he licked her lower lip with the devilish accuracy of his tongue. Leaving it burning. Tingling.

'Need more proof, *cara*?' he said, drawing back, his eyes the deepest, most sensual hazel she'd ever seen. Hot. Heavy. Glittering. The same way he'd looked at her last night. In the gardens, when he'd held her tight to his body to stem her fall and she'd convinced herself that look was antipathy. That he couldn't bear to touch her.

Suddenly the room revolved once more, spinning their situation in another direction entirely.

Dante was attracted to *her*. He felt the same way. And suddenly she was less of the girl she used to be and more Eva, the older, wiser woman on an equal footing. The woman who'd made peace with the strictures of her life. The woman who didn't need love. Nor passion. Especially with a man masterful in the art of devour-and-discard.

Oh, she'd read the tales of his jar of tattered hearts, seen enough pictures of Dante with his glamorous brunettes to fashion the ultimate armour. She may not want a relationship but hell would freeze before she slept with a man no better than her father.

So, if she was going ahead with this spurious soap opera, losing her grip, her head or her pride was not an option.

She'd been thrown for a loop yesterday, unreeling like a spool after the fund-raiser. Missing Finn, her mother. But, today, everything had changed. She had her business to save. Be the woman she'd fought to become.

If she could rise from the ashes of destruction and build a business to be proud of she could go out and be his date for dinner. Easy. Two or three dinners in a nice, controlled, professional atmosphere—deal done. Her beautiful little boutique, her new life saved. His deal saved. Everyone happy.

Some of the stress knotting her nape unravelled. Of course she could do it. She met clients over lunch, knew how to talk the talk.

There was really no need for the words *fairy tale* and *relationship* to bring on a migraine of epic proportions. It wouldn't resemble a real relationship at all. No lovey-dovey stuff. This *was* Dante they were talking about, after all.

'And this is strictly business. Right?' she asked, just to make sure they were pulling the same thread.

'*Strictly* business,' he agreed in a low, deep growl that sent a shudder the strength of 7.0 on the Richter scale on a direct course to her pelvis.

Oh, boy, if this was going to work the man *had* to keep his distance.

Conviction enhanced the adrenalin pumping through her body and Eva pushed at his chest with all her might. He didn't budge one inch. 'What are you made out of—granite? Will you back off? You've proved your point.'

He stayed right where he was and demanded, 'So your answer is?'

'Yes. I'll do it.'

'Good,' he said, pushing his weight off the sofa, the outrageously expensive silk of his suit rippling over his hard body, his face a picture of that-moment-didn't-happen dispassion as he strode towards the door. 'Get your coat—we're leaving.'

Gripping the curved lip of the sofa back, she twisted at the waist, swivelling towards the door, brow furrowed deep with suspicion. She didn't like the sound of that command. There was nothing businesslike about going out on a Sunday morning. 'What do you mean, *we* are leaving? To go where?'

'Shopping. I'm going to buy you the biggest diamond you have ever seen, *cara*. Let the fairy tale begin.'

CHAPTER FOUR

THUMB FLYING OVER the screen with speed and dexterity, Dante tapped a reply to an e-mail on one phone and pressed his second phone to his ear. Fluid French streamed from his lips as he spoke to one of his directors in Paris, conscious to the point of aggravation of the woman sitting beside him.

Quiet, subdued, Eva had barely said two words since leaving her apartment. It unnerved him. Made him want to climb into her brain. Quite a change from thinking about climbing inside other parts of her.

His thumb paused as he ruthlessly tamped down the ferocious heat pumping through his blood.

Cristo, he'd seriously miscalculated this side of his proposition. Attraction.

If he'd thought the skimpy top and gypsy skirt of earlier was synapse-scorching, it was nothing compared to what had greeted him when she'd finally deigned to exit her bedroom.

Skin-tight black jeans, knee-high boots with a

kitten heel, a white polo neck clinging to her gorgeous breasts and the sexiest little brushed suede jacket he'd ever seen, the colour of peridot. Zesty and fresh, the lime-green was a distinctive signature found deep within the earth under tremendous heat and pressure. It suited her volatile temperament and his inner state to perfection.

Jacques, his Director of European Operations, fell silent as if waiting for Dante's reply. To what he had no idea. And another flicker of annoyance sparked in his gut. With ruthless precision he ended the call and attempted to douse the flames of his ire. He didn't need this kind of distraction. What was it about the woman that made him so hot? And why did his body insist on replaying that moment back in her flat when she'd reached up… touched his jaw and sent a bolt of lightning shooting through his body?

Glancing across, he found her biting her ring finger nail as she stared out of the limousine window, a deep frown pleating her brow.

Dante tucked one finger down the back of his tie knot and gave a good tug. 'What is it, Eva?'

Hand falling from her lips, she began to stroke the leather door panel with the tips of her fingers. Without turning to face him, she said, 'I don't understand why you have to buy me an engagement ring when this isn't real.'

Dante ground his back teeth. 'To everyone else it is real. Let us not forget I was engaged to another. For this to work we are talking undying love here. The sweeping-off-your-feet variety. For this to work I cannot introduce you to Yakatani without one.' Affecting a careless shrug, he forced his voice to become neutral. 'When it is over, you may take the ring as a token of my appreciation.'

Shifting on her bottom, she turned sideways and her eyes speared darts of disgust. 'Is that what you say to all your women?'

'I'm a very generous man, *cara*.' Often he sent jewellery as a gift. They were a fond *arrivederci*, not a love token.

Cristo, he'd never given a love token in his life. Even Natalia, his father's idea of the perfect bride, had chosen an engagement ring from the Vitale collection.

The memory brought his head up from the screen. Why was he escorting Eva himself—or frog-marching her if the displeasure on her face was anything to go by? And right there he had it. Even if he gave her an unlimited credit card she wouldn't go. The woman wore sheer obstinacy for skin and she didn't *do devotion*. But at least she was honest. If he could admire her for anything today, it was the truthful delivery of that statement. Any other woman would have lied or at least tried every trick in the book to play heart's desire—such lies inflamed his gut.

While he was in no doubt that his dark, brooding looks drew them in, it was the drugging scent of bank notes—the aphrodisiac of power—that dropped them before his feet.

Eva's eyes began to sparkle brighter than the winter sun slashing through the black leather interior. 'Hold on… I have my mother's ring at home—we can use that.'

'No,' he said in a firm tone, brooking no argument. Or at least it would have, if it wasn't Eva he was speaking to.

'Why not?' she tossed back. 'It's a good idea. Why waste your money on me?'

With no intention of telling her his body simply rejected, rebelled and downright screamed *no way*, he kept the strength of his response leashed. 'I am not wasting anything. It is insurance. Suppose someone recognises it? Your father. His latest viper wife.'

'You're right. Good point.'

Dante blinked wildly in mock horror and slapped his hand over his heart. 'Say that again, *Tesoro*. I shall record it for future reference. May even convert it to a ringtone.'

'Ha bloody ha.' Turning to face front, she wriggled back into the plush padding and he noted the tiny smile she tried to stifle. One that vanished with her next thought. 'I wouldn't give her the satisfaction.'

'Ah, yes. Which number is this?'

'Sixth.'

'Has your father never heard of sex outside of marriage?' For the life of him, he couldn't fathom why Nick St George kept returning to the snake pit time and time again.

'Oh, I'm sure he has,' she said, directing her gaze back to the sweeping view of Knightsbridge, the hurt in her voice unmistakable.

Dante had never given the man much thought. Only remembered the subtle weakness that hovered over him. But sitting here, now, hearing the anguish in Eva's words, he began to question Nick St George's untimely departure and how it had affected Eva, a girl so close to her mother.

Before he knew it, his voice softened, 'I do not blame you for being hurt by the events of last night. It was beneath him to allow it.'

A new emotion burst through the sultry static crackling in the air. 'You don't know anything about my dad,' Eva said, her temper bubbling to the surface. 'So please keep your opinions to yourself. He has no control over the actions of his wife, therefore he can hardly be held accountable.'

It wasn't so much the words as her tone that threw him. She was *defending* him!

'As you wish,' he said. 'The woman certainly took great enjoyment in setting you up. No matter. The joke is now on her.'

Eva snorted. 'Oh, yes, until we break up. Then I'll be a laughing stock.'

'A *laughing* stock?'

'Oh, come off it, Dante. Everyone will think you've thrown me over for a new improved model. Who on earth would believe otherwise?'

For a moment his thoughts derailed with the nonsensical idea that she harboured a lack of self-confidence. *Improved*? How was that even possible? In the beauty stakes, she was untouchable. And hold on…

'*New*? I very rarely date women under—' He couldn't remember the last time he'd had a date, never mind her age. No wonder his legendary control was tauter than a tightrope and just as hazardous.

'You were saying?'

'I do not consider age when I take a women to

my bed.' He didn't. Did he? 'The only thing I ensure is that they know the rules.' His rules. And he supposed women in their early twenties were less complicated. They were perfectly happy with what he offered. Good sex and a lucrative farewell.

'In any case, I am older than you. Four years at least,' he said, wanting to get off the topic of sex and beds before he grabbed her small waist and hauled her atop his lap to straddle him. Then she'd know exactly what age, make and model he was currently lusting after.

'It's different for men,' she said, warming to her topic, hands wafting in the air. And Dante felt a small smile tug at his lips. She'd always been expressive. At least some things were still the same. 'Look at George Clooney. Or Sean Connery. The older they get, the yummier they get.'

His lips flattened with the speed of an express train.

Yummier? 'You find older men attractive?' What was the black emotion swelling in his chest, pinching his ribcage, making him shift in his seat? 'But you have only just turned twenty-seven.'

'I...' Head whipping round, she searched his face. 'You remember my birthday?'

November fifth. Bonfire night. How could he forget? She was born to cause havoc. 'I remember your eighteenth birthday party. The Masquerade Winter Ball.'

'Oh. No wonder you remember the season. You brought that dark-haired French actress who went skinny-dipping in the lake and almost contracted pneumonia. What was her name again?'

No idea.

'My point, Eva, is no one will believe our break-up is due to upgrade requirements. We will give a short statement to the press claiming irreconcilable differences and we only wish to be friends.'

She '*pfff*'d, the vibration rippling over her lips. 'Irreconcilable. How very apt. Except friends tend not to hate each other.'

'*Hate* is a strong word, *cara*.' While he felt a hyperbolic spin of emotions, not all of them were of the hostile variety. 'Haven't we just had this conversation?'

'Lust is different,' she said huskily. 'We're ignoring that bit. This is business. Safe.'

How long would she last without sex? If her sexual appetite were anything like his today, she would be hungry by Wednesday, famished by Friday. And on Saturday...

A flashback seared his retinas and he glanced at the blinding sun in an attempt to burn the image from his mind. Utter waste of time and effort. For still he could see her as if it were only yesterday. Eva locked in the arms of her rock star…his filthy hands fanning the upper curve of her ass. His Tequila-drenched mouth buried in her neck. Mere hours after Dante had done the exact same thing.

Bitter acid flooded his tongue. *Maledizione,* what was it with women? Why couldn't they honour one man? But hadn't his father told him this from the day Dante had walked onto the Vitale estate, no more than fifteen years old? That his own mother had been a whore just like any other.

Dante hauled air into his tight chest. He wasn't used to this wild emotional state. He was calm. Nothing rattled him. Except *her.*

Keeping his voice steady and even, betraying none of the tumultuous churn of his thoughts, he turned on her. 'It's time we discussed the rules.'

She visibly stiffened before him. 'Rules?'

'*Sì.* Rules,' he bit out. 'No provocative dress. *No* drinking. And, most important of all…you will remain faithful to me, *comprende*?'

Eva drew back, blinking over and over. And he wondered then how much of the darkness was showing on his face. 'F…faithful?'

'*Sì.* Completely. Utterly. Faithful.' Diving into her eyes, he attempted to curb the lash of his tongue but it was a useless pursuit. 'When the furore settles and we separate, you may sleep with whomever you wish. In the meantime, do not betray me. You will not like the consequences, *tesoro*. This may be business but I will not be made a fool of. Even in appearance. No boyfriends. No. Sex.'

Hot, heavy and sticky, the air clogged her throat, seared her skin and evaporated the moisture from her mouth as they faced off in the rear of the car.

For the briefest second she thought she saw pain in his eyes but this was Dante they were talking about—all cold, ruthless determination and closed off to the power of ten. Otherwise she would think the idea of her sleeping with another man bothered him. And maybe it did. Not on an emotional level but on the playing field of pride. Eva knew all about pride.

'This from the man who specialises in one-night stands and two-month marriages,' she said, wincing at the bitterness in her voice. Still, 'I would *never* embarrass you in such a way. I thought the whole point of this charade was to protect our reputations, not crucify them. Honestly, Dante, I've had enough. I am sick and tired of your caustic references. I do *not* sleep around. Never have, never will.' And wasn't *that* the understatement of the century! If he only knew... *Don't go there, Eva. Just don't go there.*

Time stretched paper-thin as he searched her face for the sincerity she prayed was there. Eventually he drew back, nodded.

The jerky reluctance in that movement didn't fill her with confidence but it was a start. 'And do I have your word that I will gain the same consideration from you?'

'*Sì*, of course,' he said, voice coated with umbrage.

'Oh, you're offended by that demand? Well, now you know how I feel. Neither of us truly knows the other, so can we stop this? Call some kind of truce. Please?'

Because surely the only way to get through this wretched charade with her soul intact was to try to get along with him. Maybe they could be friends. *Oh, yeah, when he thinks you're a bed-hopping harlot who carouses on the dance floors at night?* Like that was going to happen.

Well, she decided, she'd just *make* it happen. While he claimed not to trust her, he *was* taking a leap of faith. So this was her chance to prove to him that she wasn't the Diva, party-girl-extraordinaire. That she'd pulled her life around. And maybe, just once, he would look at her, converse with her with something other than derision. Was that really too much to ask?

Maybe it was, if the assessing scowl on his face was anything to go by.

'Dante, listen, I—' The car rocked to a stop and her attention veered to the stunning black and white façade of *the* most exclusive jewellery store in London.

Thump, thump went her heart as she soaked in the sight…the dim interior. And relief zigzagged through her body. 'It's in complete darkness. Oh, what a shame,' she said, sounding suitably disappointed. 'It's closed.'

'Good,' Dante said, face now schooled into impassivity.

Eva frowned, then jolted as the car moved forward, negotiated a tight corner and pulled down an alleyway, coming to a dead stop outside a large, ominous black door. Oh, *hell*. 'Is this the tradesmens' entrance?'

'I believe so,' he drawled with a self-satisfied smirk she wanted to swipe off his face. He was enjoying this, she realised. The sadistic snake.

A phalanx of bodyguards walked from the car behind—a car she'd had no idea was following them—and took up position standing sentinel either side of a vault-like doorway, which began to open with eerily slow precision. Eva felt as if she was watching some horror movie from behind a cushion and this was the moment where the heroine lost every brain cell she was born with and walked headlong into the temple of doom.

'Let's go,' said Dante, unfolding his long muscular frame from the car. Standing tall, he swept one broad hand down the front of his jacket as he waited for her to alight.

Except her bottom was adhered to the leather, making her feel all kinds of stupid. What on earth was wrong with her? You'd think she was walking down the aisle to wed the devil himself, not buying a *fake* engagement ring.

'Eeeva?' he ground out.

'Yes, I know. I know.' Swallowing around the lump lodged in her throat, she shimmied across, took Dante's proffered hand and plastered a smile on her face that would place the Cheshire cat in the unemployment line.

A rotund grey-haired man hovered at the open doorway, bowing to Dante with a smile almost as big as hers. Although she doubted it was costing him the same extortionate price—three years' worth of facial tightness at least. When Dante squeezed her hand with hot, virile strength and stroked a seductive circle over the plump ball of her thumb a ripple danced along her veins and she boosted that estimation to ten.

'Good morning, Edward,' Dante said. First-name terms. She should've guessed.

'Sir, it is an honour to see you again.'

Again? Oh, *great*. He must've brought Rebecca here for her *fake* ring too. Humiliation nipped her cheeks and she wished there was a crack in the paving to slither through. Being one of many was not a condition she'd ever strived for. And for some reason she wondered if her father had taken all his wives to the same shop for multi-purchase discount.

Edward welcomed them into his dark lair with quiet aplomb and Eva twisted her wrist this way and that, attempting to wriggle her hand from Dante's hold. *Nada.* So, with her free hand, she grabbed the sleeve of his jacket, tugging him back a little so she could hiss a violent whisper. 'We should've gone to a different shop. The man's going to think you're a serial fiancé!'

'I could not care less,' he said, his dark voice booming down the hall, making her wince.

'Shh.'

'Why?'

'Because…well…' Yes, Eva, *why*? If he didn't care what people thought of him, why should she?

He was so unapologetic. She should hate that, she really should. Her brain was obviously warped because she found it hot. Sexy as hell. Not a good sign. 'You're right,' she muttered so only he could hear. 'Who cares if you escort two fiancées here in one week?'

They were shown into a large lounge area, the walls adorned with sensual boudoir-type prints that sent heat, fast and furious, coursing through her body. *Oh, boy.* What with the erotic red walls, enormous black velvet couches, seductive mirror-top tables and the low crystal chandeliers bouncing shards of shimmering light off every surface, she began to wonder if this place sold more than jewellery. Never in her life had she seen such carnal opulence. It was seriously evocative, yet bizarrely romantic. Dizzyingly so.

'I want a diamond, Edward.' Dante's unyielding command knocked the air from her lungs so, by the time he encouraged her to sit upon a velvet sofa, she could do nothing more than obey with a slump. Dante shot her a quizzical glance as he sat beside her.

Too close. *Oh, boy*, was he trying to sit on top of her?

'I want the most beautiful diamond in the world,

Edward. For the most beautiful lady, wouldn't you agree?'

'Absolutely, sir.'

Oozing deference, Edward slid a small tray in front of them and Eva's eyelids fluttered as sweat prickled behind her knees. She inhaled a deep stuttering breath.

'Eva?' Dante said, a tinge of concern in his voice colouring the question. And still she kept breathing, trying to work out what was bothering her so much. The room? Dante?

Then his scent—so dark, so rich—drifted up her nose, wrapping around her senses, so when he nuzzled her neck she curled her face towards him with a basic instinct. Wanting to be closer. To relieve the need pulsing through her body, thrumming against the lace of her knickers.

Dante dropped an open-mouthed kiss on the sensitive skin between her neck and shoulder… tugged gently on her earlobe with his front teeth— flooding her core with liquid heat—and whispered in her ear, 'You are the first woman I have ever brought here. I often buy specialist stock from Edward for retail. There is no need to feel embarrassment, *tesoro*.'

Heart thumping, she eased back a touch, slowly opened her eyes and locked them on to his beautiful dark depths, glittering with sincerity. His recognition of her embarrassment was around ten minutes too late, but it was something, wasn't it? 'Okay.' *Pull yourself together, Eva. Think temporary torture, long-term happiness.*

Content she was back in the game, she moved her attention to Edward's small smile, to his assistant—a pretty, elf-like blonde—who heaved a long blissful sigh behind him.

'See anything you like, madam?' Edward asked.

Eva scanned the selection of diamonds. Huge, whopping diamonds. Ovals, squares, pears, hearts—blurring into one huge white nothingness, much like the pit of her stomach. Where were the price tags? How did she know if he could return it?

'No.' Dante's unimpressed voice shot through the haze. 'Too plain.'

Edward nodded his assent, lifted the tray from the table and swivelled on his heel.

Dante slipped his hand between the tight slit of her clenched thighs and she nigh on jumped off the couch. Had to bite her tongue to stop from yelping. Because, honest to God, she was sure that awesome body of his could fuel the energy supply for an entire nation.

'Relax,' he said, silky, sinful. 'You are too tense. Choose what calls to you.'

Another tray. Another pad. More diamonds. More carats than Lexi, her old precious mare, would munch through in a week. None of them called anything except *run*, gallop for your life. 'You choose. I don't care.'

Dante's fingers bit angrily into her inner thigh for one, two, three beats of her cantering heart.

'Scharrt,' he ordered with a calm severity that fired another burst of hot tingles through her bloodstream.

A small feminine gasp rent the air and Eva glanced at Edward, whose eyes lit with unabashed delight. *Scharrt.*

Excitement enhanced the crackling atmosphere, so she knew it had nothing to do with spreadsheets—they were the most boring things in the world. Whereas Dante, the financial genius probably got off on them. Another difference. Another divide. Another reason she'd never have been enough for him all those years ago. Compared to Finn and Dante, Eva's B grades made her intellectually challenged.

The elfin blonde began to vibrate as a crushed velvet pad the colour of midnight appeared in front of Dante. One fleeting glance and Eva's heart stopped. Dead.

Edward's voice came to her as if spoken from

the other side of reality. 'The stunning emerald-cut yellow diamond with trilliant-cut white diamond shoulders. Totalling thirty-eight point one carats. One of rarest diamonds in the world, sir.'

Dante picked up the ring, took her hand from where it lay fisted on her lap and uncurled her fingers with a gentle stroke. *This is not happening. This is not real*, she repeated inwardly, fighting the tremble starting in her toes and meandering up her legs, spiralling through her midriff.

Dante slid the heavy platinum band along her finger, nudged it over her knuckle and embedded it deep. 'Perfect fit,' he murmured.

Perfect. It was perfect. From the cool platinum band to the sparkling diamonds flanking the shoulders to the biggest, most beautiful stone she'd ever seen—the most gorgeous rich shade of yellow. It was the ring of fairy tales. Of handsome princes and happy-ever-afters. It was the ring a man gave to the woman he loved beyond reason. It was for her clients. It was *not* for her. Because the gesture was as cold and empty as her stomach, whose pangs she felt every time she looked at it.

Breakfast. She must be starving. That was what this was all about. She needed to eat—

'We'll take it,' he said.

'No!' Hand shooting to Dante's thigh, she

gripped his honed flesh, felt it tense beneath her fingers. Felt the answering fizz in her blood. Ignored it.

The notion that she was supposed to be play-acting came a second too late and she scrambled for a ditzy *oh, gosh* look and turned towards Dante with a flirty coyness she hoped she remembered how to pull off. 'What I meant was…it's too much. You don't need to prove your…' She couldn't say it. Love. It was a total, utter lie. She, who loathed lying, was living a lie. Lying to everyone around her. 'It's not right.'

Dante gave her an admiring glance that said her *performance* was Oscar-worthy and sank his hand into the nape of her neck. The touch of his fingertips against her scalp… The way he tugged her to him with ferocious need… *Oh, boy.* And then his breath shimmied over her tongue as he spoke against her lips, just loud enough for everyone to hear. 'Nothing is too much for the woman of my heart, *tesoro.*'

Another blissful sigh came from…somewhere. Realisation hit and her eyelids fluttered closed. *Oh,* he was seriously good. And she'd never hated him more. Or maybe she had. Yes, yes, of course she had. When he'd left her in the pool-house, promised he would come back. Swore he wouldn't leave.

Yet he'd disappeared into the night like a dark phantom. When she'd needed him the most. Just like her father had left her mother.

Self-preservation knocked the pain from her chest and she twisted her head to speak low in his ear. 'I'll get you for this, Vitale.'

Drawing back, he loaded up that mouth with enough sex appeal to slay half the female population, snagged her hand and swooped up from the couch.

'Send me the bill, Edward.'

Yank, he tugged her down the hall in his wake. As far as social development went, it was one touch away from clubbing her over the head with a mallet and tossing her over his shoulder. Not that she cared. Speed was definitely of the essence.

Fresh and crisp, December stung her face but it was sheer bliss to Eva and she tore her hand free and darted towards the car door being opened before her.

From nowhere one steel arm blocked her way and suddenly Dante stood smack bang in front of her. 'Ready?'

God, yes, she wanted out of here. Away from him. What planet had she been orbiting when she'd agreed to this loony scheme? It was possibly the stupidest idea in the universe. *Temporary torture.*

Long-term happiness. Just remember what type of man he is—a predator who devours and discards.

'Yes, I'm more than ready,' she said. 'And if you think for one minute I'm going through this again—'

'Good.'

Slam went that full sexy mouth over hers, obliterating her every thought and dropping her headlong back into the inferno. Heat doused every inch of her, soaking her in his blistering formidable power. The ground whipped from beneath her feet, her heart flipped over in her chest and, with one touch of his warm tongue against hers, she was riding a demon wave of scorching lava.

Anchoring herself, she reached up, vaguely noticing the strange weight on her left hand as she speared her fingers into his gorgeous thick hair. And, *oh, boy*, he tasted of sex and sin and dark bitter chocolate. He tasted of Dante. Of everything she remembered and more. More power. More strength. More passion. More. More. More.

Lips slanting, firm and lush, he devoured her mouth with long, leisurely licks, leaving her restless, breathless.

Maybe she closed the gap, maybe he did, but suddenly they were flush-tight, silken-clad iron crushing her breasts, steely fingers dominating…

gripping her nape, keeping her to him, as if he never wanted to let go. As if he wanted her, wanted her so much.

And suddenly, with the same speed he'd lunged for the kill, Dante loosened his grip and Eva rocked back on her heels, swaying on her feet as the earth spun and lights exploded behind her eyes.

'Perfect, *cara*,' Dante said in a voice that solidified the heat in her midriff to a block of ice. 'That should do very nicely. Now we can be *certain* of what we will wake to find tomorrow. And let's have no more talk of the need to *fake* anything.'

CHAPTER FIVE

'ARE YOU HAPPY now, Vitale? Once again, there I am. Smack bang on the front page!'

Eva's voice shot down the phone line and would've easily burst his eardrum if he hadn't been holding the phone ten inches away. 'Good afternoon to you too, *cara.*'

'Don't *cara* me. You set me up!'

No, what he'd actually done was set *himself* up for an endless night of physical torture.

Dante surged from his leather chair and, palm flat to the chilled glass, braced his weight against the vast window of his UK headquarters. The unrivalled views of a festive Mayfair were doing an abysmal job of assuaging the tension snaking through his ribcage.

Where the hell was the Princess of the Press? Why wasn't she revelling in the attention? It was almost as if she hated it.

'What is the problem, Eva? It worked, didn't it? Are the reporters free from your doorstep? *Sì.*

Have they soaked up every drop of exaggerated mulch? *Sì*. And let us not forget how you appeared to get into the spirit of the thing.'

Cristo, that was an understatement. The woman was a siren, hell-bent on his destruction!

'Yes, well, anyone would've got into the spirit of the thing when dealing with an expert in the field. Just *look* at me.' He was looking at her. Filling the front page. All long black sculpted legs and thick caramel hair cascading down her spine, five seconds away from having sex on the pavement. 'I'm all over you like a sticking plaster. Finn is going to get the shock of his life. Please tell me you've spoken to him, explained that it's all a…a lie.' What was it with the woman and lying?

'There are no lies between us on that page, Eva.'

'I'm not talking about the lust and you know it. I'm talking about the engagement.'

Dante paced the fifty-foot length of his office. 'No, I haven't spoken to Finn. His line is still down.' And, knowing his best friend, he'd be taking advantage of being snowed-in with the latest starlet to fall for his charms. At least one of them was getting some kind of satisfaction, he supposed.

'Oh, God, I hope he's okay.' The concern in her voice snagged at something deep inside him.

If there was one thing he could say about Eva,

she adored Finn with all her heart. At one time that sibling loyalty had made his chest clench with envy. For, after being wrenched from his mother's pitiful grave and dropped into the opulent world of Primo Vitale, his father's legitimate heirs had been consumed with hatred.

Not that Dante had cared. After a childhood spent in a squalid, debauched hell, he'd been darker than sin himself and ready to take on the world. Little had they known it would be Dante who would save them all from financial ruin. It would be Dante who now held power in the palm of his hand, able to crush their world at will.

'Dante, are you still there?' Eva's voice, rich and decadent, washed over his taut, hard body in soft lulling waves.

'*Sì, cara*, I am here. We are talking about a man who drives at the speed of light. It will take more than snow to knock him off course.'

Her soft breath whistled across London as if she tried to be calm, to believe. 'You're sure?'

A small smile curved his lips. 'I am convinced Finn is safe and well. But, if it makes you feel any better, I will contact one of my men in Zurich to search for word of his team.'

'You will? Oh, well, I'd really appreciate that. Thank you.'

Dante stiffened his spine, smoothed his hand down the front of his tailored jacket and hauled his thoughts back to order.

'Good. Now that is settled and you have calmed—'

'I have not calmed. And I'm not finished with you yet either.' Ah, there it was. The tongue of a vixen. That husky voice. Every sex-dripping syllable wrapping around his groin and pulling tight.

'I see you have found your voice today.'

'My brain is what I've found. First off...no more kissing,' she said, more than a little breathless.

It was a good idea. Also impossible. For two reasons. One, this charade must go on. And two, it was becoming impossible to keep his hands off her. Luckily, this time next week, Hamptons would be his, her deal with Prudence West would be saved and he'd be jetting to the Far East. Out of sight, out of mind.

'Are you listening?'

'To every word,' he replied, scrolling through his e-mails to see if there'd been any word from Yakatani.

'I don't believe you. Put your phone down. I do realise I'm a mere female but I want your undivided attention when I say this.'

'Say what?' he murmured, distracted by the incoming fist to his gut in the form of a text from his half-brother, Lazio—one he deleted without reading and moved on.

'No more fake loved-up flower arrangements. No. More.' Her voice cracked and his eyes sprang up from the screen. For a second he imagined she was struggling to breathe, to talk, but when she spoke again her sass was full throttle. 'It's one thirty and my boutique resembles the Chelsea Flower Show.'

'You do not like flowers?' he asked incredulously. Women adored flowers. Usually in every colour and variation. Maybe she was a lingerie girl… He stopped before crashing into another wall of lust. Never in his life had he bought a woman lingerie and he wasn't about to consider the notion now. Especially with a woman he'd never get to see modelling it. Torturing himself with self-denial he was not.

'Hate them,' she said tightly. 'Although I must admit it's a recent development.'

'How recent?'

'This morning recent.'

Dante settled back in his chair, the leather cushioning the blast of affront. So she didn't want his ring. She didn't want his kisses. And now she hated flowers because he'd sent them. A unique state of play, to be sure. Still, he assured himself, if Eva was so opposed to romance that was her problem, not his.

'Now that's sorted,' she said, 'I have to work. So I'll see you Wednesday for dinner with Yakatani?'

Leave her *alone*? For two days?

'I think not, *tesoro*. Until my name is on Hamptons' deeds, think…sticking plaster.'

Eva smoothed her satin sheath down her front, snagging on her oddly heavy left breast and winced.

Hormones. Nothing more. Nothing less. What with the ring and the lust, and the flowers and the lust, and the kissing and the lust she was in a volatile state. Add in the fact the man couldn't seem to leave her alone and she was a wreck!

Monday evening, Dante had demanded dinner at a fancy hotel, where he'd spent half the time on his phone with some Russian oligarch. Tuesday evening was the Scottish Ballet premiere, which in any other circumstances she would've adored. But she'd fallen headlong into the inferno on the red carpet beforehand and the flaming heat had burned bright for the entire performance. By this morning she'd learned her lesson in the art of submission and tied herself up in so many appointments he couldn't demand lunch.

Now all that was left was dinner tonight. Yakatani, Dante and Eva. Easy. Private. No kissing. With a bit of luck he'd close his deal and leave her in peace.

Sucking in air, she pressed the flat of her hand to her stomach. Stomach ache. Every day. All day. *It's hormonal. It's the kissing. You know this.* But, *oh, boy*, the kissing. Made her want more. Of him. Of that sinful mouth. Not only humiliating, considering the man was made from the same cloth as her father, but it was all for show.

Oh, yes, the devil had the entire British press wrapped round his pitchfork. Every day there they were, front page headlines. It was awesome to behold and, though she was loath to admit, it was far nicer seeing captions professing devotion than detailing the latest 'Diva Scandal'. Even Prudence West had agreed to meet her on Friday to discuss 'everything' and she was *not* blowing it.

Grabbing her long crushed-velvet coat from the back of the couch, she checked the clock before sinking her arms into the cool silk lining and buttoning from neck to knee. The long hand clicked to the hour and Eva heard the rumble of a machine so loud the building shook as if she lived beneath an airport.

Lights off, she walked to the living room window to see…*wow*, a blood-red Lamborghini Aventador parked outside the boutique. The coveted super-car, named after a famous bull, riding double yellows.

The air whooshed out of her lungs as the sexy-as-sin machine open its jaws and Dante unfolded his tall muscular frame from the low-slung seat.

Thump, thump went her heart when, with a deft flick, he shut the car door and fingered his yummy hair. More with frustration than for appearance's sake.

Then her knees turned to water as he ate the pavement like a black panther, all deadly, lithe masculine grace. Dynamic. Energised. And *outrageously* sexy.

Mouth dry as hessian, it took her a few seconds to realise what his intentions were.

'Oh, no.' The place was a tip!

Quickly, she grabbed her vintage ruby-red clutch, rushed to the front door, swung it wide, moving forward a pace, and slammed straight into his chest.

'Miss me *that* much, *tesoro*?' he said, voice dripping with sin as he curled his fingers around her upper arms to steady her.

'Like a hole in the head.'

He pursed his lips as if containing a smile and before she remembered the sinful flavour of that mouth she backed up a pace, clutching her handbag to her chest. 'Shall we leave? Don't want to be late for the big event.'

His hot gaze trailed down her body, lingered on the flare of her hips…her bare calves until she felt positively giddy.

'What have you got on under there?' he drawled, for what felt like the hundredth time this week. 'And…' his eyes lit with fury '…*where* is your ring?'

Oh, *great*. 'I forgot, I was in a rush—just give me a second.'

'You *forgot*?'

Eva breathed deep, fighting off the need to punch him in the arm. Knowing her luck, she'd break her knuckles. 'What are you getting into a tizz about?' If she didn't know any better she'd say he was offended. 'It gets tangled up in my hair in bed and…'

Eva glanced at the crimson plaster wall of her hallway, seriously tempted to bang her head off it.

'You—' he croaked, before clearing his throat '—you wear it in bed?'

She couldn't look at him—she just couldn't. 'I tend to play with—' *Oh, boy*, was it too much to hope the floor would crack open about now?

'Play with…?'

Eva swallowed. 'My hair. In my sleep.' This was awful, awful, awful. 'I'll get it.'

About turn, she headed for her bedroom, his footsteps echoing on the oak behind her, the snick-ity-click of the front door closing. 'Just stay there. I'll be one minute.'

In she went, out she came. Took one look at his dark, thunderous face. 'I'll check the lounge.'

'*Cristo*, I realise it means very little to you, but how can you lose a ring in a day?' Was it her imagination or was there a thread of hurt in his voice? 'When tonight is the night you need it most!' No. Not hurt. He was angry as hell.

Light splashed over the room and she winced at the ivory threads worming across the carpet, the sewing paraphernalia littering every surface.

'*Maledizione*! You expect to find it in *here*?'

'Of course I will. Come on, don't you ever put things in a place where you'll never forget? Then forget?'

'Oddly enough, no.'

After a few minutes, Dante joined in and from nowhere the memory came to her and she strode over to the black mantelpiece. Halfway there and she snagged on Dante digging his hands down the sofa cushions in case it had fallen from the arm. And her stomach plummeted to the floor. 'Stop!'

Dante froze, slowly straightened to his dizzying full height.

'There it is,' she said, one unsteady finger pointing to the mantelpiece. 'I remembered. Told you I would.'

Insides shaking, she prayed he'd walk away. He could *not* see those papers from the specialist. He'd want an explanation and she couldn't lie and he'd tell Finn and Finn would worry and maybe tell Dad and *oh, God*, she had to get him out of here. Distract him somehow.

'Come on, I'm starving,' she said, practically shoving him out of the door. 'Where are we going, by the way?'

'Takumi,' he murmured, distant, suspicious.

'I think I read about that in the papers.' *Keep talking, just keep talking.* 'Some spectacular star-studded opening.'

'It's Yakatani's new venture. Or should I say his son's. Takumi is the Michelin chef taking the country by storm. Tonight is the opening.'

Eva stalled halfway down the hall. 'I thought this was dinner. Me. You. Him. Private.'

'It is dinner,' he said, now exasperated. Which was fine. It was better than being suspicious. 'And getting to private is the goal here. It is an honour to be invited. Meeting informally is the perfect launching pad.'

Yeah, to fire her off to the moon.

'Think you could refrain from kissing me on the carpet tonight?' It was a stupid request. Because, from the look on his face, she'd just waved a red rag to a bull.

CHAPTER SIX

A LINE OF super-cars and limousines snaked a path to Drathon Tower, sitting on the bank of the River Thames, soaring into the sky, all black tinted glass and subtle curves.

Dante watched Eva lean forward, head tilting to peer up through the windscreen as the parking attendant waited for his signal.

'What were you saying about this meeting being the perfect launch pad? It looks like a rocket, don't you think?'

It looked phallic to Dante but he was beginning to think his mind was continually in the gutter these days. Or at least since Saturday when this little missile had projected into his life.

Cristo, never had he spent so much time with one woman—*hell*, with one person. And the sight of his ring on her finger, stamping his possession all over her slender hand, only made him even more aroused. Knowing she wore it to bed, that she touched herself, caressed all that beautiful almond skin with *his* ring on her finger only turned up his internal temperature gauge.

Any other woman and she would have been flat on her back by now. But she was still Finn's little sister and there was no way he was crossing that line for a fling, however heady, however sexually gratifying it would be.

What was more, she was hiding something. Being secretive. Sneaky.

And, just like that, his temperature dropped through the red leather bucket seat. He'd missed the signs with his ex. Although he often wondered if he'd cared enough to look. But right now, with Eva, there was too much riding on this deal.

After motioning the parking attendant to open his door, he walked round to Eva's side and took her small hand in his.

'Wow, I'm getting the full treatment tonight,' she said.

Whether it was her sassy mouth that sparked his fire or her repeated request not to kiss her, he wasn't sure. But his mood darkened with the desire to put on a real show. The devil in him wanted proof that she could no more resist him than he could her.

Gripping her hand, he hauled her from the seat—knowing every lens was focused upon them, that thousands of eyes would see the stamp of his possession—and brought those lush curves flush against his hard body.

Fisting his jacket lapels, her wide green eyes shot up to his. 'Dante,' she whispered frantically, 'what are you doing?'

'Not on the red carpet, Eva, that was your request.'

Plink. Plink. Bright white camera bulbs saturated the air in a dazzling display and Dante plastered her against the glossy carnal-red paintwork and took her mouth on a joyride she'd never forget.

It took him a good few seconds to think past her brazen lips frisking over his and the heat pervading his groin, to realise his fatal error. This was Eva and the woman kissed him as if he was her last breath. All sex and desperation. So he tangled with the uneasy notion that it would be *him* who would never forget. When business should have his undivided attention. That Hamptons was the goal here.

Even the imprint of her hot mouth refused to leave him as they rode the glass express elevator, zooming up forty-two floors in complete silence, Eva refusing to meet his eyes and Dante fighting the destructive animalistic need to pin her against the steel cage. *Business, Vitale—focus.*

By the time they were greeted by the maître'd he had the hunger leashed…until Eva's long black velvet coat slipped from her provocative body and his heart stuttered in his chest.

Cristo…

Swathes of golden silk sheathed her body like a second skin, from the high slashed neck to the straight cut knee in an understated oriental elegance, the wide band cinching her waist embroidered with delicate pink orchids and tied at her back in a huge gold bow.

Sensually extravagant. Yet oddly demure.

He had to swallow in order to speak. 'Eva, *cara*, you look…'

'What?' she asked warily.

'Stunning.' Like thwacked-over-the-head stunning. 'Breathtaking.'

Her high cheekbones flushed crimson. Another hint of innocence. As if she'd never been given such a compliment in her life. Which was ludicrous to imagine in a woman with a trail of ex-lovers in her wake.

And thankfully, before that thought took hold, they were ambushed by Takumi and it was back to business. To safety. To total control.

Together they worked their way through the throng of foodies, TV personalities and society's usual glitz, nibbling on sushi and tempura, while Eva sipped an odd concoction of lime and lemonade—to satisfy her sweet tooth, he was sure. And, when they were shown to the private cordoned-off table of Yakatani, Eva dipped her head and greeted the older man in stilted Japanese. Making Dante rock back on his heels. And that was just the beginning of tonight's stun-gun attack.

Every time their upcoming marriage was mentioned she blushed that intoxicating rouge that swept down her neck and all he could wonder was if it covered her gorgeous full breasts. Yakatani was smitten with her apparent innocence. But the more Dante watched her, the more he suspected it was untruths. At one point she stumbled so hard, Dante had to catch her fall.

Turning to his host—a small man in his greying years who reeked money and intelligence—he asked, 'So tell me. Are you looking for a quick sale?'

'Yes. The quicker the better. It is time for retirement. My wife informs me she would like to see her husband before he meets his maker. As you can see,' he said, encompassing the glass and steel extravaganza with a sweep of his hand, 'my children all have their own interests.'

'It's spectacular. You must be very proud of your son.'

'Immensely.'

Dante couldn't mistake the sincerity and a fist of envy punched him in the gut. One he stiffened against. Pushed past. Moved on.

'Any issues with the store I should be concerned about?' Dante asked.

'Just the usual. Concessions getting complacent. Staff issues. Nothing that a man of your reputation cannot handle, Vitale.'

'New blood.' Eva's voice drifted across the table and, when Dante looked up, her attention seemed divided between their conversation and Yakatani's daughter-in-law, who'd just settled into the chair beside her, all long straight ebony hair and sloe eyes. Or was it the baby in her arms—a boy, if the blue sleep suit was anything to go by.

'You were saying, *cara*?' he said.

Her head snapped around, soft blonde waves swishing about her shoulders. 'Oh, sorry. It was just when you said…concessions.' He could feel her reluctance and it reminded him of the times she used to put herself down in the intellectual stakes during conversations between themselves and Finn. Not that Finn helped one iota. Without realizing, he'd used to make Eva feel as if her opinion didn't matter. It aggravated Dante. He knew too well the frustration of not being good enough, worthy enough to be heard.

'Go ahead, *cara mia*. We wish to hear.'

'Well…in my opinion, you need new blood. A better mix of class and sass. In the ladies department especially. The problem is your rents are too high and so you're not allowing the up-and-coming designers a chance to exhibit their raw talent. London is the place they want and they can't afford it.'

Dante blinked.

Yakatani's smile reached his deeply lined eyes and he said, 'What would you suggest, Eva?'

Warming to her subject, her hands joined in the party. 'Free rent for six months to get them established. Then off they go into the big wide world. Or they have the money to start paying *you* rent. Now, before you get all hot and bothered—'

Hot and bothered? *Cristo*, he was burning up.

'—about the words *free rent*, think about what you would gain. Respect in the industry. The opportunity to showcase new stars, thereby bringing in new custom, and satisfaction that you helped a fledgling company. Everyone's happy,' she said with another little shrug as her eyes flickered back to the baby.

Eyes that melted at the sight. Almost…longing.

With the back of her finger, she reached up and smoothed down the baby's soft cheek. Once. Twice. Dusted over his dark mop of hair with a loving touch.

Then, as if she sensed he watched her, she turned towards him and curved her beautiful lush lips. Untutored. Pure. *Affectionate*?

No. Impossible. Women didn't look at him with affection. They looked at him with lust. Lust for sex, money, inordinate power.

So Dante didn't want to think about what that smile did to him. All he knew was Eva belonged on the stage.

All too soon, her lips fell, together with her eyes. 'Excuse me,' she said. 'I must use the powder room.'

It was Yakatani's voice that tore his gaze from her lush hair and curvaceous behind.

'She is more than ready, Vitale. You will not have to wait long.'

Dante frowned. 'For what?'

The man laughed as if they shared some private joke—one which Dante wished he was in on—and said, 'That has certainly made up my mind. It is time we brought this discussion around to its lucrative assets. I fly to Tokyo on Friday and will not be returning for two weeks, so time is the issue. I prefer a quick sale, if you can manage it.'

Dante eased back into his chair, back in control of his world. 'I also fly east on Friday morning to Phang Ton.'

'They say it is truly a sight to behold. The most luxurious private domain in the world.'

Dante's killer instinct snarled and sniffed the scent of victory. 'I say you should see for yourself. Come. Be our guest for the weekend. Eva would love to meet your wife. One hour of business, the rest pleasure. I guarantee you'll fall in love with my slice of paradise.'

'We would be delighted.'

Dante smiled on a swell of gratification.

Come Monday morning, Hamptons would be his.

Eva stared at the first fall of snow dusting every step, every paving stone, like crystal sparkling, blazing like diamonds beneath the glare of streetlamps, as snapshots flickered in her mind. The beautiful baby boy. Dante staring at her with a dark, fierce intensity. One of his stunning ex-lovers kissing him on the cheek as they'd left. All reminding her of the naive, foolish girl who'd once made castles in the sky. Making her feel as fragile as the snowflakes kissing the heated windscreen. *Don't do this, Eva. Just walk away.*

'…so I agreed to fly out at ten a.m.,' Dante declared. 'I'll pick you up at eight. A warmer climate will suit.'

Warmer climate? Eva whipped around to face him. Noticed the car was parked outside her boutique. 'I'm not with you.'

'Have you listened to a word I said?'

She gave her head a little shake. 'Sorry, I'm tired. Tell me again.'

'Which is why you need a break, *cara.* Yakatani has accepted an invitation to my island this weekend. We fly out Friday morning.'

Eva blinked, her bones freezing despite the warm gush of the air-con. 'I can't go anywhere on Friday. I have a meeting with—' Her brain clicked into gear in the nick of time. She had an arrangement to see Prudence West. To save her deal. Her business. *All* she'd ever have. But she couldn't tell Dante that. Because all week he'd been insistent on meeting Prudence with her and she knew it would be an unmitigated disaster. Not only couldn't she think straight around him, this was her deal and she was saving it by herself. *Her* way. So, instead, she said, 'With a client.'

'Eva,' he said, the first flicker of annoyance firing his words, 'if all goes well, Hamptons is mine. It is one weekend. That is all.'

An entire *weekend*? No. *No*! No more. She couldn't take any more. 'I can't fly anywhere, Dante. I have a meeting at nine-thirty.'

'So change it.'

Eva locked her teeth, breathed deep. They'd made a deal. Yes, she wanted him to get Hamptons. Of course she did. But she was also sick and tired of him controlling her every move. 'No. I can't and I won't. Why don't you change your flight?'

'*Cristo*, cease with being difficult, Eva! I cannot go back on my word.'

'Oh, but I can? So it's okay for me to look un-professional but not you.'

'I did not say that,' he bit out, raking his hand round the back of his neck.

'Yes, you did. Can you stop thinking of yourself for one solitary second? That,' she said, pointing one unsteady finger at the façade of her shop, 'is all I have. While you stockpile billions, that little boutique is all I have.'

'So you intend to go back on your word to me? For a prospective client who you could meet when we return? *Cristo*, I knew I shouldn't have trusted you.'

'You can trust me! But we're supposed to be in

this together. You never consult me or I would've told you. I couldn't think of anything *worse* than spending the entire weekend with you but I made a deal and I intend to stick to it. We'll just have to compromise. Okay?' Even as she said the words, her stomach cramped with dread. An entire *weekend*?

Two whole days of kissing and touching. Craving the impossible.

Dante just looked at her as if she'd lost her marbles. Maybe she had.

'*What*?'

'Have you ever heard of the word *compromise* before?'

'I do not think so,' he said sardonically. 'It makes my brain slur, which leads me to believe it is a foreign language.'

'And here I thought you were multi-lingual.' She ignored the insolent arch of his dark brow. 'Compromise is when each side gives up something in order to reach a consensus. It is not me kowtowing to you. I'm quite happy to try and move my appointment back to nine but anything before that is a downright unsociable hour to call on someone. So, Mr Control Freak, if you'd like to engage in the foreign concept of compromise, you know where I am.'

And with that Eva burst from the car, slammed the door and held her head high as she negotiated the slippery foundations that were now her life. Another two days of this charade would bleed her heart dry.

Once inside, she tore her coat off, slung her bag on the sofa and paced. After two lengths of the room, an angry shrill broke her stride and she glanced down at her phone. And let loose a sigh.

Snatching the phone, she plunged into the wing-back tartan chair. 'Hello, Dante.'

'Is eleven-thirty enough of a compromise?' he said, frustration lacing his voice with that yummy accent.

Eva closed her eyes. Her body at war. Brain screaming she was getting in too deep. Heart demanding she stand by her word. 'Yes.'

'Then you'll come with me?' he asked, a little huskier.

'I will.'

Silence stretched her already fragile composure and her head fell back, pillowed, comforted by the soft warm cloth. 'Goodnight, Dante.'

'*Ciao, cara,*' he said, low and delicious. Bone-melting to the point of exasperation.

Tossing the phone back on the oak coffee table

with a resounding clatter, she released her breath in a long calming rush.

Why did he keep throwing her off balance? Why couldn't he stay arrogant and unbearable? Why did he have to tell her she looked exquisite when there was no one around to hear him? No audience to play to. Encourage her to speak, hang on her every word as if he truly cared what she thought.

A sweet sharp ache pierced her chest.

Lies. All lies. He was playing the perfect charade.

And yet, for several beats of her heart, they'd shared one long loaded look and she was eighteen again, her mother well and life was wonderful because Dante had burst into their world like a dark storm to whip her body and mind into a frenzy of want and need. And she'd taken every look, every innocuous word and spun them in the spinning wheel of her mind to weave the perfect spell— dreams of a forever kind of love. Where he'd be her first, her last, her everything.

Dante Vitale had been The One.

Then…suddenly her world had begun to fall apart. Suddenly her mother had been fighting for her life. Suddenly they'd been crushed by lies and betrayal and Eva had been catapulted into reality. Where women were fleeting diversions. Disposable. Dispensable. Where Dante soared to stratospheric heights, indulging in one-night-stands with his striking svelte brunettes, Eva knowing she could never compare.

A groan—pained, hers—echoed through the room. Because all it had taken was his warm hand reaching for hers as her mother's coffin was lowered into the ground and she'd forgotten all about how she was *nothing* like his other women. Only craved his touch, ached for him to still be her first, knowing it was her last chance…

Disaster. One she couldn't bear to remember. Because she'd start asking herself questions. Like: why? Why kiss her with the fervour she'd longed for, only to stop? Disappear. She must've disappointed him. Somehow.

Much like her second attempt at a physical relationship.

After that, she hadn't needed any more proof that she wasn't made for sex. So, in reality, when she'd been told she was high risk, the decision to avoid men altogether had been easy enough to make.

But now he was back.

Dante Vitale, the only man who'd ever made her feel true desire, was back.

And if he'd been disappointed five years ago, God only knew what he'd think now. Now she was broken. Racked with fears even she struggled to comprehend.

She didn't want to want him. To lie in his arms and be held, desired, made love to with a dark thrilling intensity. So why, every night, when her flesh was stone-cold and the silence was a physical ache, was she dreaming of that with him? *Still*, after all this time.

Impossible.

It was all too late.

One more weekend. Then this charade would end and she'd find peace. The desire would wane. It had to.

She'd forget him again. She must.

Right now it was time to save her business. All she'd ever have. And she was doing it *her* way. The only way she could live with herself.

She was telling Prudence West the truth.

CHAPTER SEVEN

SLEEK, SOPHISTICATED, AND as sexy as its billionaire owner, Dante's white super-yacht sliced through the mangroves, trailing ribbons of white froth in its wake.

Hair whipping about her shoulders, spray slapping against her skin in a refreshing cool mist, Eva basked in the endless beauty before her—towering rock faces on either side scored by the hands of time, the rugged façades sprawling with greenery and delicate ivory flowers she couldn't quite place.

The sun was sheer bliss, a blazing orange, rich and soothing against a sky so blue it could only be described as God's blank canvas.

Paradise on earth.

'Comfortable?' Dante asked, a savage edge still lingering in his tone. A censure she ignored. Yes, she'd been running late for the flight but the man was lucky she was still standing after the week she'd had.

'Very comfortable, thank you,' she replied, all

sweetness, determined to lighten the mood, if only to get her over the next two days, as she lounged back in the buttery white leather chair.

Despite his dangerous aura, Dante leaned insolently against the back of the dark wood helm facing her, his tall muscular body draped in tailor-made trousers the colour of crème bisque and a navy blue polo shirt—all suave class and sophistication.

Arms crossed over his glorious wide chest, her eyes seared over the densely corded muscle of his forearms before gliding to the open neck. Navy collar flipped high; the crisp edges flirted with his hair but it was the aviators wrapped around his face that almost tossed her over the edge.

Even after all these years, working with models, hanging out with the most handsome men in the world, Dante was still the most savagely beautiful picture of masculinity she'd ever seen.

Tearing her eyes from virile perfection, to her glass of freshly squeezed passion fruit juice, to the sheer beauty whistling by, she said, 'Oh, how the other half live.' It was meant to be a joke, a compliment. Instantly, she knew her mistake.

Dante's lips twisted. 'You've been cushioned by wealth all of your life, Eva. Still would be if you hadn't blown your mother's legacy on the party scene.'

Hand tucked into her side, Eva clenched the folds of her white sundress. 'How do you know about my legacy?' Blown on the party scene? My God, he really had a low opinion of her. Insides twisting, it took every ounce of effort to hold his slashing glare.

'Finn told me,' he declared.

'I forget how close you two were. Still, I'm surprised he told you something so personal yet you had no idea about my business.'

Something close to guilt washed over his bronzed complexion as he glanced to the east. 'It was a long time ago. The information was not freely given. I asked him if you were provided for. That is all. We have never spoken of you since.'

Grateful for the huge sunglasses covering half her face, she tipped her face towards the sun. *What were you hoping for, Eva?* That he would ask about you because he cared? That he couldn't help himself. Just as you couldn't resist the temptation of hearing one word about him?

Silence stretched, pulling her nerves every which way, until the boat swerved around the rugged edge of a cliff face…

'*Wow*! That's your island?' Clear aqua water

lapped at sand so white, so fine, it reminded her of icing sugar. Shallow beaches framed with lofty palms swaying to and fro in the slightest breeze. And, set back within dense foliage, an enormous multi-level mansion, stucco walls, wide panoramic windows. 'I've never seen anything like it. Anything so stunning. So…dramatic. Dropped smack bang in the middle of paradise.'

'Welcome to Phang Ton.'

The way he said it… 'Phantom.' Like a dark shadow disappearing into the night. 'It suits you.' One minute here, gone the next. Leaving a hole as huge and devastating as his home. But not this time. This time there'd be no shadows lurking in her world, taunting her at night.

After the longest flight of her life, she was back in the game. He would have Hamptons in his hand even if it killed her.

All she wanted was for him to look at her with respect. True respect. If they could be friends, she would have closure on the past. Move on. This was her last chance. Because after this weekend she could never risk seeing him. Ever. Again.

The boat veered into a wide private dock where a phalanx of security and staff lined up on the highly polished deck. Dressed in white, they stood to attention, welcoming their master back into his powerful lair. And in that moment she felt a ripple of unease curl around her vertebrae, shimmy down her spine at the thought of the days to come. A role she'd never undertaken before—the role of hostess to a man who demanded perfection—and Eva was far from perfection. If this past week had stretched her acting abilities to the point where her nerves were fraying under the pressure, she just hoped this weekend didn't tear her apart.

Two long, hot days of sailing and scuba-diving in the glorious depths of the Andaman Sea blurred into nights of cocktails, laughter, dinner and dance. And by Monday evening, as Dante stood on the deck and waved Yakatani and his wife goodbye, a tidal wave of satisfaction washed over him.

Knowing Eva was waiting for him out back, he swivelled on his heel and jogged up the tiled steps, swerving into the staff entrance at the side of the house. After snagging a bottle of champagne and two platinum-lipped flutes, he headed back outdoors, this time veering left to skirt the balcony to the rear where the fresh scent of the island's jungle-like interior hung in the vaporous air.

One look and Dante took the usual swift kick to the guts.

There she was. Standing beneath the terracotta-tiled canopy gazing at the lush foliage, one hand twirling the tiny pearl at her lobe, the humidity clinging to her almond skin. Dressed in a white short-sleeved broderie anglaise shirt and a matching knee-length flirty skirt, she appeared angelic. A vivid contrast to the untamed danger surrounding her.

Lowering the chilled bottle to a small table, he noticed the pensive expression on her face and his heart did a strange pang.

Clearing his throat in warning, Dante watched her spin around, her face brightening as she walked towards him.

'Well?' she said, coming closer, caramel locks bouncing about her breasts, her gaze darting over his face. 'Stop teasing me. What did he say?'

Either she was emotionally invested in this deal or her acting skills were outstanding. Because he wasn't sure, he tried for an unconcerned shrug. 'Sign in two weeks.'

Fire, fierce and instantaneous, lit those stunning green eyes. 'Yes!' she whooped. And flung herself into his arms, or maybe he picked her up—*who cared?*—because he locked his arms tight around her and swirled around the floor. 'I'm so happy for you,' the words unnecessary because the way she kicked her feet into the air as he took her lush weight said it all.

Dante buried his face in her hair, inhaling the scent of camomile, so pure, so soft, so innocent.

A mass of emotions assailed him. That was why he held her tighter still, rocking, trying to block the image, the memory, the sudden question in his mind—one he'd *had* to stop asking himself a long time ago...

Why? Why had she run straight into the arms of another man mere hours after they'd parted in the pool-house? He wanted to know. Why? Why she'd acted so desperate for one night with him when any man would've done? But what was the point of dredging up the past, only for her to deny what he knew to be the truth. He wasn't even sure he could say the words without showing the unwelcome force of his emotions. What a fool she'd almost made of him.

Arms going slack, he gently lowered her to the floor and when she'd gained her footing he took a giant step back.

No matter the past, there were things she deserved to hear. 'You were amazing, *cara*. Made quite the impression. Yakatani has invited you and me to stay in Japan whenever we wish.'

Cheeks pinking, she smoothed the hug-wrinkles

from her blouse with unsteady hands. 'Oh, dear. How did you get out of that one?'

'I didn't. I had more important things on my mind.'

'Like?' she asked.

'Thanking you.'

A warm smile—small and sweet, untutored and beautiful—curved her lips. As if he'd reached to the sky and plucked a star, just for her. 'You're welcome,' she said quietly, that sense of melancholy returning—one he couldn't understand, one he wanted to erase.

'Come,' he said. 'Let's celebrate. I have a bottle of the finest fresh from the cooler.'

While Eva held the glasses up, Dante had to force his eyes to do their job until the amber effervescence bubbled to the platinum band, in one, then the other. After sliding the bottle back to the table, he took one glass and toasted, 'To the future of Vitale. The biggest retail phenomenon in the world.'

'Congratulations, Dante. I hope it brings you much happiness.'

Happiness? Hell, no, his memory was too good for that. Still…

Clink went the flutes as the finest crystal collided in mid-air. 'Grazie, *cara*.' Years of hard work to ensure Vitale was crowned the world leader. To prove he was worthy of the name. That he, the bastard heir, had succeeded in doing what no other man had.

Tart and smooth, the cool liquid fizzed over his tongue, popped and crackled down his throat as he watched Eva from the corner of his eye. Simply cradling the glass. The exact same thing he'd watched her do all weekend.

'Why aren't you drinking?'

'I don't drink alcohol. But that doesn't stop me toasting your success.'

Dante's face twisted in disbelief. 'Eva. Come, now. I spend very little time in London but your antics were enough to reach news-stands the world over. Photographs, too many to count, you and...' *Your lover.* What was wrong with him? Why couldn't he even say it? '...Van Horn. Other male friends besides. Drinking. Partying. *Exclusive* clubs.' The words began to fire out of his mouth like bullets because suddenly it wasn't Eva he could see. It was his mother. Stumbling through the door, yet another man in tow. Another noise from her room. Part pain. Part pleasure. Dante covering his ears with the palms of his hands...

Bile rose in his throat and he swallowed, over and over.

'I know how it looked,' she said, her hesitant voice pulling him from the depths to meet a sense of shame hovering in the air. 'Believe me, I know. And I can blame the press for exaggerating my every move. For painting me the Diva. But I was the maker of my own downfall. I put myself in their path. I knew what I was doing at the time. Or at least I thought I did. In hindsight, I think I was…lost. Searching for what, I don't know.'

Dante blinked, bringing her face back into focus. There she was. The Fallen Angel. But at least she could stand tall and admit her mistakes. Had his mother ever done that?

'The paparazzi bothers you now.' Because she had a reputation to protect. So the Diva he'd expected had failed to make an appearance.

Now she lived only for work. Just as he did. She'd turned her life around and he admired her for that. Yet, there was more. Beneath. Secrets. A contradiction in her life he couldn't grasp.

'It always has. But this week, for the first time in my life, I haven't felt controlled by them.' One side of her lush mouth curved and the temptation to lick and taste made his mouth water. 'No, instead I've been controlled by you.' She placed her glass of amber fizz on the table. 'Reminds me of that adage: from the frying pan into the fire.'

'Too much heat, *cara*?'

'Way too much,' she said, edgy, breathless. Avoiding it. Fighting it. All they'd done all week.

And, *Cristo*, this weekend. Sweat-drenched nights of wanting, knowing she was in the bedroom opposite his. Those long satiny legs tangled in his sheets. That creamy almond skin smothered in his finest silk. Her breasts pushed into his soft mattress. His ring on her finger.

Of course the constant craving only served to heighten his frustration and fury. How could he still want her after she'd betrayed him?

Eva sat on the top wooden step leading down to the tropical interior. 'Anyway,' she began, slipping the black wedges from her feet and poking her toes into flimsy white tennis shoes, 'you promised me a walk on the wild side and, before I leave in the morning, we need to decide when we'll officially break up.'

The flute froze halfway to his lips. He watched the golden bubbles nudging, popping against the glass while his lungs remembered how to breathe. The reason, he assumed, was because they were nowhere near done.

Dante drained the glass in one smooth swallow. 'Let us not think of that now. We have two weeks until I sign and Miss West to contend with.'

Eva's foot froze mid-wiggle and she tilted her head until thick caramel hair tumbled, veiling her face.

A loud drum beat throbbed at his temple. '*Eeeva*? What are you not telling me?' Secrets—he could feel them lingering, putrefying, thickening the air like poisonous gas.

Eyes wide, determined, obstinate, locked on to his. 'My meeting on Friday morning was with Prudence West. She's going elsewhere for her gown. I lost the job.'

'*What*? I've a good mind to call the woman and tell her what a disastrous mistake she is making. Why did you not wait for me?' *Cristo*, why would the woman not let him take control?

'I can fight my own battles,' she said quietly, padding down the wooden steps to negotiate the beaten path snaking a trail through the wild tangle of palms, ferns and towering tree trunks.

He almost told her she hadn't fought this one very well but in that instant something dawned on him. Something so profound the earth revolved three-sixty. Pretty much the same way he felt every day this woman had been back in his life!

'And yet,' he said hoarsely, launching down the steps, his loafers crunching the woody undergrowth, curling his fingers around her upper arm, he tugged her to a stop, to face him, 'you came here regardless. When I could do nothing more for you. For two days you have entertained, been the perfect host, bewitched Yakatani at every turn to persuade him to sell to me. *Why*?'

'Because I gave you my word. You wanted Hamptons so badly and I wanted you to have it. Why shouldn't one of us win?'

Bang—another shot from that stun-gun of hers—like a poacher's bullet straight between the eyes, making his head jerk. Never in his life had anyone done anything so selfless. Only for him.

Rendered dumbstruck, he found himself in the unique position of not knowing what the hell to do about it. And yet…as his eyes dipped to where she licked her full lips, there was one thing he'd never been more certain of in his life.

He wanted—*needed*—to kiss her. More than his next breath.

Except wasn't it more likely that Eva *needed* something more important than a taste of the man beneath?

In that moment Eva wouldn't have changed the last week for anything and, considering her entire life, her career, her business was hanging in the balance, that was saying something. But it was glorious to see derision replaced by a bud of admiration and a whole load of shock.

There was something else, too. An incredible force of will tautened his hard frame as if he leashed raw power. And the air began to pulse and moan as blood rushed through her veins.

Before she did something very stupid, like jump back into his arms to be held deliciously tight, beg him to kiss her and never stop, she stepped back and resumed her walk down the rutted pathway, shaded by the lush green overhang.

Without the Duchess, she had no idea what would happen next. All she knew was that she needed to wrest back control, call a halt to this charade, fly back to London and try to rebuild her world pre–Dante Vitale. Again.

Goose pimples flurried up her arms and she shivered violently.

Dante snapped out of his odd stupor and fell into step beside her. Voice controlled, so dark she sensed a danger in him, 'I'll make up what you lost on the job. It is the least I—'

Heat flamed from within, licking her insides, firing her voice. 'Don't even say another word. I wouldn't take a penny of your money. It was my choice to go it alone. Anyway, I had every intention of telling her the truth—'

He coughed an incredulous bark. 'The *truth.
Maledizione*!'

The reason for his outburst suddenly dawned on
her and her feet screamed to a halt. Swivelling to
face him, she reached out a placating hand, careful not to touch, knowing she was at the very edge
of her control. *Don't touch him, Eva. You'll lose
your mind.* She knew. Just looking at him set her
body on fire. *Oh, boy—focus, Eva, focus.*

'Hey, don't worry, okay? I realised at the last second how it may affect your deal and I didn't tell her
in the end.' There she'd been, sitting in Prudence
West's morning room being congratulated on her
and Dante's engagement, and Eva had frozen, lies
clogging her throat. Knowing there was a good
possibility she would be risking his deal. So she'd
sat there and told more lies for a man. One thing
she'd *sworn* she'd never do after her father's antics.

In the end it had been pointless because, 'The
decision had already been made.' And Eva had
no doubt the soon-to-be Duchess had been pres-
surised by the cliques. One of which was fake
fiancée number one—Rebecca. Eva had known
from the start the power of a woman scorned. But
Dante had his eyes on the prize and what would a
man know of such humiliation, such pain? Noth-

ing. 'My point is, I either make it on my own to swim or—'

Whoosh, he was off, dark, primitive and perilous, garbed entirely in stark, uncompromising black, pacing in front of her like a predator at home in his habitat. 'Are you telling me you will sink without it? So why will you not take my money? What the hell kind of woman are you, Eva? *Cristo*, first it is the ring, then the flowers, now my money! Am I not good enough for you, is that it?'

Good enough? Was he serious? Did he even know what he'd just said? No, surely not, he was too angry.

'Calm down. It's not personal. I won't be bailed out by anyone. I have new consultations lined up.' She just hoped they still came off when the novelty value of her and Dante wore off. And she didn't even want to think of what would happen when their break-up was announced. 'I won't sink. I've made it this far without help.'

Punching his fists into his pockets, he sent bark flying into the air with the toe of his loafer. 'Bank loans,' he growled, as if he knew. But she guessed his financial brain just connected the dots.

'One or two,' she choked out, trying to make light of her situation around the block in her windpipe. If he knew the true astronomical amounts involved he'd be…well, much like he was now—exasperation oozing from his every sinuous pore as he held her with an intense slashing glare. But that was ludicrous. He couldn't possibly know.

His pulse-thrumming physique towered over her. 'Are you telling me, you actually frittered over eight million on the party scene, to be left with *nothing*?'

So much for avoiding this topic of conversation. 'Don't be silly, Dante. On a couple of club memberships and a few parties? Only you could think that way in the first place.'

'So what happened to the money?'

The first prick of a migraine stabbed behind her eyes and Eva rubbed her temple. 'My dad remortgaged the house over and over. We almost lost it. I couldn't bear to see my mother's pride and joy being sold. Funny thing is, I can't even bear to go there now. To watch his latest wife tear another room down. Another strip of silk from the wall. By the time he'd settled on wife number four, my legacy…my car, Lexi…was gone.'

'*Maledizione*! You sold Lexi, that pampered mare, the love of your life, to keep your father in that house? Finn *allowed* this?'

He was practically ranting. She couldn't help but smile. 'Finn was racing in the F1 World Championship at the time. When he came back he was furious, but it was too late. In all honesty, he doesn't know half of it. He already worries. Feels guilty. So don't you *dare* tell him. It was my choice to bail my dad out. And I'm sure you realise how much ex-wives cost.'

A thick, turbulent storm clouded his beautiful eyes. '*Sì*. I know this.'

Eva questioned how wise it was to pursue such a conversation. She couldn't bear to imagine him with his ex-wife. It physically hurt. The svelte brunette must've been infinitely special to coax Mr-One-Night-Wonder down the aisle. 'I'm guessing once was enough for you.'

'More than enough,' he said fiercely. 'And no, I do not wish to talk of it.'

Meaning there was an underlying hurt. Strange to imagine a mere woman having the power to hurt him.

'So you loved her?' she asked, wincing inwardly at the crack in her voice.

Dante choked out a laugh. A horrid, mocking sound that sent the tree-dwellers into a flurry of squawks and scuttles. 'I am incapable of such a thing. Love is for the weak and needy and I am neither.'

No, he was neither of those things. He was all

indomitable strength and power. Always had been. Always would be.

Dante scrubbed his hands over his face, raked his hair with his fingers. 'Eva, I refuse to stand back and watch you struggle.'

'You have no choice,' she said with a hard undertone he couldn't easily miss.

'*Cristo*, there must be something else you want. What if I buy your lease? Move you to Mayfair. Buy you a house. *Whatever* you want. As a thank-you for closing this deal for me.'

Growling, she flung her arms wide. 'Is that your answer to everything? *Money*?'

He gave an insouciant shrug—an act that completely contradicted the sudden tension emanating from his powerful frame. And words, *his* words, began to prick her psyche. *What the hell kind of woman are you, Eva? Why will you not take my money?*

That was exactly what he thought. Women only wanted him for his money. It was the most hare-brained notion she'd ever heard and yet he *actually* believed it.

A sweet, sharp ache pierced her chest. How must that feel to him?

In truth, she knew. How many times had she wished people would see past her notorious pop star father, her uber-talented mother, even Finn, the dashing, death-defying racing driver and see *her*, Eva? Want to spend time with *her*, Eva. Not that she could get them backstage passes or get them smack bang on the front page, or even a longed-for introduction to Finn. And to think that all this time Dante—*the* Dante Vitale—felt something similar, just boggled the mind. Cracked her heart.

Forgetting about all the reasons she wasn't to touch, Eva reached up, brushed the back of her fingers down the side of his savagely beautiful face, cupped his unyielding jaw. Felt the heat and need trickle through her veins. Ignored the desperate surge of self-preservation to pull away. Because he *needed* to hear this.

'Oh, Dante, I don't want your money. I knew you when you had nothing.' *I wanted you when you had nothing.* 'And still I don't want or need anything from you.'

Brow scrunching, he gave a flummoxed shake of his head, eyes never leaving her gaze, those haunted, almost tortured umber eyes boring into hers as if searching for veracity.

Veracity he must've found because that look morphed into something hot and heavy and thick. Clouding his eyes with hot, devilish intent. Clawing the air with ferocious need. 'Now *that* is a lie,

Eva, and you know it. You wanted something from me then and you still do…'

Daunting and more than a little dangerous, his voice incited a weft of excitement and a warp of unease through her body.

'…A taste of the dark side.'

Oh, boy. Hand slipping from his face, she took a tentative step back, heart thundering so loud she'd swear a herd of elephants were stampeding towards them. *Run, Eva, run.*

Except his deep gaze held her captive as he towered above her in an unmistakable pose of sexual dominance. Then his big strong hands shot to her waist and yanked her flush against his hardness.

'Let me go,' she panted, even as she gripped his upper arms, felt the dense muscle flex beneath her fingertips, sending a deep tremor through her core, exploding in a feverish flurry.

A ghost of a smile played about his sinful mouth. 'Say it like you mean it, *cara*, and I will consider it,' he said in a voice thick and syrupy with hot, sweet intent, sucking heat from her every pore to gather and pool low in her pelvis.

Oh, hell, did he have to be so…so horridly, deliciously male?

Eva cleared her throat, tried again. 'Let. Me—'

Pounce—the fiend jumped straight in for the kill

and nipped the words from her bottom lip with his front teeth. And when he soothed the tingling flesh with a sinful flick and lap of his tongue the jungle vanished behind her eyelids. *Think, Eva, think.*

'Explosives. Dangerous. We're ignoring this bit, remember?'

Except now he was doing that nuzzling thing that turned her brain to a cotton puff ball. That delicious, delirious, nuzzling thing, where he brushed up the side of her face with his roughened jaw and the erotic friction made everything go maddeningly wild inside her.

Breathe, Eva, breathe.

'I've had enough of ignoring it,' he growled. 'It makes me angry.' He licked the sensitive skin beneath her ear and inched his way down her neck, tasting her skin with delicious, dewy, open-mouthed kisses, and the sensory overload sparked the need to thrust her fingers in his hair and hold him to her. So tight. So close.

His big hands curved around her waist and moulded to her bum before he yanked her tight against him and slanted his mouth over hers in a kiss of seduction and fire. And, *oh boy*, she could feel him, hard against her stomach, and she rolled her hips against the thick ridge of his erection, desperate now, mewling against his lips.

His answering groan coalesced, fogging the air with a carnal cloud. '*Cristo*, I *must* have you, Eva.'

The thought that she was in the jungle, being ravished by the king of all predators, should have had her scrambling up the nearest tree but, *oh boy*, she'd never felt so alive. He really, truly, seriously wanted her. And she wanted him to take her, devour her. With all that dark, delicious, smouldering power. Just this once.

Her heart wasn't at risk. She wasn't that girl any more. As long as he didn't stop; she couldn't bear it if he stopped again.

'You kiss like a flaming siren, you know that?'

She did? Ah, well, it didn't take a genius to work out what he'd expected. A siren to drag down, down, down into his inferno. Such heat, she would surely burn.

Eva. A siren. If she wasn't on the scorching cusp of the mother of all orgasms she would laugh. Because surely she would disappoint him again. Of course she would. *Oh, boy*, what was she *thinking*?

'Dante, I…should go pack. I leave early and…'
I'm scared. In case I can't be the woman you want.

But this is your last chance, Eva, your only chance to have him. Inside you. To know what passion truly feels like. To know what Dante Vitale feels like.

His grip tightened with a sharp possessive nip as he thrust one hand into the hair at her nape, curled the other underneath her bottom and lifted her into his arms, encouraging her to wrap her legs around his waist until her lace knickers snuggled against his hard, thick length and a helpless plea poured from her throat.

'The only place you are destined to be, *cara*, is in my bed.'

CHAPTER EIGHT

UP THE SWEEPING grand staircase they went, while Eva snatched kisses, nibbling, biting her way across the scimitar curves of his hard cheekbones and jaw. When she thrust her hands in the hair at his nape and tugged at the silky strands, Dante sucked air between his teeth, his low baritone a sonorous boom, '*Cristo*, Eva.'

Stumbling awkwardly, Dante paused on the first landing and crushed her against the wall to deepen the kiss and press hard up against her. *Yes, kiss me. Kiss me. So I can't think. Don't stop. Please don't stop.*

The notion that it would be quicker to let her walk filtered through her lust-deranged mind but thankfully he seemed to share her urgency because off they went once more, down the wide picture gallery hallway to their suites, lips locked, banging into the walls, first one side—knocking a priceless painting off its perch, the clatter caroming around the cavernous space—then the other, time and time again.

Slam went her bedroom door against mink plaster, then *slam* back it went, before Dante loosened his grip and Eva slithered down his body, luxuriating in every wickedly hard inch of him.

Lungs screaming for air, their lips tore apart but the onslaught never stopped, not for one second.

For a seamstress, her fingers were failing miserably, fumbling with his shirt buttons and after a good five seconds she tore it wide.

'Hungry, *cara*?' he rasped.

'Famished.' She could do this. Definitely. Be everything he expected and more. Hadn't she read enough steamy books in her time? Of course she had. Hadn't she been Oscar-worthy this week? Of course she had. With any luck, enthusiasm would more than make up for the fact that she was about as practised as a nun. Because there was no way on earth she was disappointing him again.

Eva smoothed her palms over his chest, the thin dusting of hair over his honed pecs, her palms burning. 'You're so hot.' Feverish.

'Always for you,' he said. Injecting her bravado with another shot of intensity.

Snap went the button on his trousers and Dante kicked them to the floor—*don't look down, don't look down, you're bound to blush like a gauche fool*—before he curved his big hands around her waist, stopping at the small of her back to whip down the zip of her skirt.

Eva felt the cool fabric swish down her legs, his fingers curl under the waistband of her knickers, and fought another bout of antsiness that she was nothing, *nothing* like his skinny other women by crushing his mouth with hers, tangling with his tongue in a raging sensual dance of wills. Thrust, parry, back and forth, heads slanting for a deeper connection that spoke to her very heart.

'Next time we go slow, *si*? I've waited for you too long,' he said, unsteady hands back at her stomach, fumbling with the thin belt of her blouse. '*Cristo*, it feels like an eternity. I want you, Eva. In my arms. In my bed.'

Eternity? Eva closed her eyes, knowing he didn't mean it, but it sounded so wonderful she took every word, locked them in her mind. Just as she'd used to all those years ago. Little meaningless things he'd said to her or the way he'd said her name. She'd store them all. Knowing it was wrong, bad for her soul.

'It's okay,' she said breathlessly. 'Whatever you want.' Because the way he wanted her, with such desperation, drowned out the voices, warning, whispering.

He whipped off her belt and unsnapped the tiny hooks down the centre of her blouse, opening the material wide and smoothing his hands to ease it over her shoulders until she stood only in her white lace bra.

Before he could even think about taking it off, she lunged back to his mouth, lips clashing with a hunger he returned tenfold.

Dante backed her towards the bed, his hands around her back, reaching for her bra clasp and, dammit, she felt her shoulders stiffen, her stomach pull with a fear she'd never been able to understand. But it was so strong, she undulated her torso, rolled her shoulders to dislodge his hands.

Thank God he didn't seem to notice and they plunged atop the bed, Dante's glorious weight pushing her deep into the sumptuous, luxurious swathes of satin and silk.

'Eva, what the hell do you do to me? *Cristo*, I cannot think.'

His hands were everywhere. In her hair, fisting. At her waist, gripping. At her thigh, lifting her leg high over his hip. Wildfire trailing. Skimming over her bottom. Then she felt him. Hot and, *ohh boy*, he was huge and thick, and she widened her legs, hoping…hoping…

But then his hand followed the dip of her waist to cup her breast and her insides chilled, grew taut. No. *No!* She tried, she really tried to breathe, to relax, but at that moment she realised her mistake. She should've told him. Told him everything. And that realisation made her tense even more. Because he would never have believed her. Never.

Too late. Too late, she knew.

Lips locked, he groaned into her mouth, his huge body flexing and then *slam*, he drove inside of her with one powerful thrust.

Her insides tore as if wrenched with a red-hot darning needle as he embedded himself so deep she'd swear he crushed her heart. Arching her spine, she couldn't stop the high-pitched cry spilling from her lips, pouring over his tongue.

Blackness hovered at the edges of her mind, dancing around with her vision, skewing her pulse. And she tore her mouth free. Dragged air into her lungs. Gasping. Gasping. *Don't you dare pass out, Eva, don't you dare. Breathe. Breathe.* In and out. Slow and even.

Glimmers of warm sensation—like dust motes—fluttered inside her. A heady feeling of rightness—blissful, halcyon rightness—seeping, easing, until she grew lax and smoothed her hands over Dante's shoulders.

Shoulders that were locked. His honed body the epitome of a cast bronze god.

Eva prised her eyes open, eased back, looked up…

And her heart stopped. Dead.

Horrified. He was utterly mortified. 'Dante?' she whispered, hating the tremble in her voice.

'No,' he choked before cursing thickly, words slurred by his heavy accent, '*No*! Impossible.' His damp dark hair clung to his temples as he shook his head, lifting his weight, his warmth, his protection, from her body.

'Stop!' This man was *not* doing this to her again. 'Dante, *please*. Don't do this.'

The past slammed into her, throwing her back five long years, and there she was, lying on the sofa in the pool-house, clothes torn in haste—*Stay with me, just tonight.* If not to give her the night she'd always dreamed of, then just to hold her. Tell her everything was going to be okay. That the pain would diminish somehow. And he'd stood up. Left. Walked away. And she'd lost him too. Leaving her so alone, so lost, she'd drifted mindlessly for months, years.

A tear slipped, unchecked, trickled down the side of her cheek into her hair. 'Please don't go.'

Same look on his face—stupefied, stunned, blinking as if waking. As if someone or something else had taken over his body and he was fighting it. Fighting it with all his might. Struggling. Struggling for control.

'I… *Maledizione,* Eva, I cannot.' Same words, same darkness falling into his beautiful eyes as he withdrew, disappeared into the black of night. Never to be seen again.

Palms flat, Eva pushed his chest. 'Just go, Dante,' she said. 'Just…go.'

A deluge of feeling, as if he'd been doused, plunged into a thick, turbulent whirlpool of emotion, had Dante yanking at the mocha satin sheet and draping it delicately over her body as she buried her face in the pillow and curled onto her side in a defensive ball.

Scrunching his eyes shut, his guts twisted so hard the muscles in his stomach gave way. Abs crunching, he flinched.

Cristo, he'd hurt her.

Control obliterated, he'd been riding on the atavistic need to take her, make her his, stamp every other man from her mind. Mindless, desperate, he hadn't even removed her bra and he'd taken her with the civilised finesse of a savage barbarian.

Dante tore his eyes from her, whipped his hipsters up his legs and took another swift punch in the gut when he saw pale red smear the white cotton.

An innocent. *Maledizione*!

Another swirl of thick black emotion curled in the pit of his belly, one he'd never known, and it made him feel sick and his heart ache.

He stalked through to the en suite bathroom, bent over the tub and twisted the gold taps until water gushed, hot and steamy, pooling generously at the base. Tearing through the mirrored wall cabinets, he found the bath soak he'd ordered especially for her, tried one squirt, gained ten little bubbles, so he tore off the lid and upended the entire bottle with a satisfying squelch.

Plumes of neroli flower and gardenia wisped in the air and Dante strode back into the bedroom, around the side of the huge bed, sank his arms underneath her prone form, swept her up in his arms, holding her tight, so tight to his chest as he carried her through.

'Dante?' she breathed, tensing, struggling for a few heart-tripping seconds until she burrowed into

him, curled her arms about his neck. 'Wh…what
are you doing?'

Slowly, inexorably, he eased her into the water,
wincing inwardly as he waited for her pained cry.
Yet she just looked at him. Green eyes sparkling
with *amazement*?

She'd expected him to walk away. To leave her.
As if he cared nothing for her.

Rubbing over his chest with the palm of his hand,
he asked himself: could he really blame her for
thinking such a thing? *You're cold, Dante, hard,
just like your father, how can anyone love you?*

Brow lined with pain, Dante watched her lift her
knees and hug them to her chest. And it was right
then he noticed the soaked white straps…

'*Dannazione, cara*, your bra, I forgot.'

'Oh, it's okay,' she said, her attention drifting to
the mass of scented bubbles rising around her. 'I
have another one.'

'Here,' he said, bending over the roll-top to reach
her back. 'Take it off.'

'No!' Jerking her shoulders to stop him. Dante
swallowed hard. She didn't want him touching her
and could he blame her for that either?

'*Cristo*, Eva, why didn't you tell me?'

She shook her head in a sweet, naive kind of
sadness and the ground gave a peculiar tilt. It was

like looking at young Eva. As if the clock had been turned backward. As if the last five years had never happened.

'I thought you wouldn't believe me,' she said.

And that feeling came back. Made him want to do strange things. Like get in that bath. Snuggle up behind her and hold her and rock her and wash away the blood, the pain. But she didn't want his touch, did she? No. So he rooted his feet to the floor, knowing he didn't deserve to assuage his own needs, and stood firm, his every muscle aching, burning under the pressure.

'I'm okay. Honest. It was just a flash...at first. It was almost gone.'

'It was?' he said, releasing a breath he was unaware he held.

'Yes. There's no need to feel guilty. It wasn't your fault.'

Guilt. Yes, that was what he felt. Guilt. Fault. Because it *was* entirely his fault.

Wasn't it?

Maledizione! A lightning bolt shot down and every muscle in his body coiled with murderous intent.

'*Cristo*, that bastard told me he'd had you six ways till Sunday.' Lies. Lies. Lies Dante had believed.

Eva's head snapped around. 'Who? Who told you that?'

Dante thrust his fingers through his hair. 'I cannot have this conversation with you naked.' Except for the bra. There was something…something not quite right about that bra and he couldn't work out what.

And *hell*, all he wanted to do was get in that bath. He'd be lucky if she ever shared one word with him again, never mind water. And just the thought of never touching her again, tasting the sweet delicacy of her skin, devouring her lush mouth. *Cristo*, what was wrong with him? He was losing control, dammit! 'Ten minutes. Then I will be back.'

'*What*? You can't drop that bombshell and then leave me. Dante, wait!'

Ignoring her sassy mouth that said if he walked out he wouldn't get back in again, Dante stormed to his bedroom, showered, donned some black lounge trousers and stalked back to her room. Half-expecting it to be locked.

The door was ajar; he eased it open, his chest clenching as he found her standing in front of the dark wood dressing table, tearing her hair out with a soft paddle brush. 'The only reason you're back in here is because I want the truth. I deserve it. Then you can leave.'

Slap went the brush to the dresser as she turned to face him, sparks firing from her eyes, swamped in a fluffy white robe, arms crossed tight over her breasts in self-defence.

Dante cleared his throat. 'Are you sore? Do you need painkillers?'

'I'm absolutely fine. I want to know who said that about me.'

Raking his hand round the back of his neck, he said, 'Van Horn. The night of your mother's funeral. After you and I…parted in the pool-house.'

Silence seeped into every crack, every fibre, except the corners of his mind, where he could still hear Van Horn's vile words. Still feel the blistering fury that had almost smashed the other man from Kent to kingdom come.

Expecting her temper to flare, instead he found the green depths of her eyes swimming in hurt. 'And you…you *believed* him?'

Truth. Always truth. '*Sì.* Every word. He told me you'd been an item for weeks.'

'Weeks?' she said. '*Weeks, Dante?* You actually believed that I'd had the time or the desire or even the inclination to have secret trysts and slum it in his seedy hotel rooms on tour when my mother was ill? When I'd put my life on hold to look after her night and day?'

He nodded, well aware that, for the first time in years, he was feeling something close to shame. 'I never thought of it that way. I was angry.'

'I don't care how angry you were. How could you think that of me? I asked you to spend the night with me. I—' Stricken eyes flaring with dismay, her arms fell to her sides. 'Oh, my God. You must've thought I wanted one night with you, just so I could go on sleeping with him too. That… that's sick. Disgusting. Please tell me you didn't think me capable of that?'

'I thought exactly that, Eva.'

Crushing her lips together, her thick eyelashes fluttered closed, brow pinching.

Within seconds he was padding across the mahogany floor towards her, swerving round the foot of the bed…when she snapped out of her sombre state and held one palm flat, breaking his stride a couple of feet from her.

'Why? Why did you think the worst of me? Or is every woman a conniving wretch?'

Dante faltered. He didn't suppose he'd had the greatest example of women from the start. His mother could never have been termed a paragon of virtue and admittedly his father gave him little chance to forget it. Toss in a glut of women who had their third eye focused on the scintillating lure of his billions and his cynicism had been nailed. Of course, as she'd rightly pointed out earlier, Eva had come along before he'd made his fortune. And since the moment he'd first seen her till the night he'd walked away he'd truly believed she was an angel. So why? *Because just looking at her scared the hell out of you*, his conscience whispered.

Locking on to her gaze, he said, 'I saw no reason for him to lie.' As the past unfolded in his mind, he felt a stab of retaliation. 'And don't you *dare* play the innocent with me, Eva. At the time I didn't think you knew your own grief-stricken mind. You were Finn's little sister, for Christ's sake. I came back to explain why you and I could *never* happen and what do I find? You and Van Horn locked tight in the garden, bringing new meaning to mouth-to-mouth. Before I left he took great pleasure in extolling your sexual escapades. So, from where I stood, you were quite happy to seduce another in my place.'

Her robe, so soft, so white, rose and fell on shuddering breaths and she stumbled back a step as if he'd slapped her with the sins of the past.

The usual lush green of her eyes turned bleak and she nodded. 'He found me in the maze. I was so upset. You just…disappeared. He hugged me. And yes, he kissed me.' The inner torment scouring his soul must've shown on his face because she reached out, her hand quivering in mid-air. 'But when I realised what I was doing, I pushed him away. Told him no. So I can't understand why he lied to you.'

'Come now, Eva. Can you not? The man obviously wanted you for himself. Let us not forget you were then pictured with him continuously during the year that followed.'

With one hand, she reached up and gripped both sides of the robe, closing the small gap—knuckles bleaching—hiding the thin sliver of almond skin.

'We hung around in the same crowd. Parties. Concerts. Perfectly oblivious. He persisted... hounded. Was relentless in trying to get me into bed.' Chin dipping, she looked to the floor, where she flexed her foot, rubbed her toes on the rug. 'Pity I wasn't worth the effort.'

Flinching on another swift kick to the guts, he tried to speak through the fiery knots in his throat. 'Things developed between you?'

Backing up another pace, widening the gap, she leaned against the wide panoramic window. The soothing rouge hues of sunset cast her in an ethereal light, picking up the golden strands of her beautiful long caramel hair, outlining her lush body to stunning effect.

'About a year after I last saw you…' Which would have been around the time he'd got married, he was sure. And why could she not look him in the eye? 'I decided it was time and I tried.'

'*Tried* being the operative word, *tesoro*. Because, right then—' he said, pointing to the rumpled sheets with an unsteady hand, 'you were still just as innocent as when I first laid eyes on you.' And hadn't it always been there? A whisper of purity that called to him—a man who had seen the darkest, most tainted, debauched side of life.

'I struggled. He said I was…' Closing her eyes, her brow creased and she banged her head gently off the glass.

Crack went his knuckles as his fists screamed bloody murder. 'Eeeva?'

'Sexless. He found it quite amusing that men drooled over me. Over my chest.' Cheeks pinking with a heart-wrenching embarrassment, her attempt at a small smile bordered on apologetic. 'Problem is, I don't like them being touched. I didn't realise how strongly I felt until that night. So, as you can imagine, it was a disaster. But, looking back, I agreed to sleep with him for all the wrong reasons. I didn't want him. I wanted…'

'Wanted what, *cara mia*?'

'It doesn't matter any more.'

Frustration snaked through his chest. The need to push her for more coiling in his throat. But she was closing in on herself, withdrawing. Pain pleating her brow. Making him wonder if this was the first time she'd relived it.

'Speak to me, *please, tesoro.*'

Rubbing her temple, she said, 'It was my fault, Dante. Everything he said was right. That I was a tease. I didn't mean to be. I was just messed up. He said I was frigid and his face, my God, he was so angry and nasty and—'

Black and thick, fury poured through him. 'Did he touch you? Hurt you? Make you cry?' Teeth bared, he let out a low growl, struggling to leash his temper as he sorted through words, let loose a few Italian expletives. 'That bastard. I'll kill him.' Not even close. Doubting there was a vile enough word in the Dante vocabulary that could come close to satisfying the noxious mixture of frustration and rage that churned through his veins.

Eva's eyes flared wide and she pushed off the window with her bottom, laid her hand on his upper arm. 'No, no, hey, you can't do that! He just said nasty things. That's all. In all fairness, Dante, it was true. He couldn't even—' She looked down at his crotch. Seemed to stay there a while. 'You know.'

'He couldn't get it up, right?'

Tipping his head to one side, he snagged her attention from the thick ridge in his trousers. 'Let me make one thing abundantly clear, Eva. That excuse of a man was probably so high on drink and drugs that he could not stand up, never mind get *it* up.'

Insanely, he was grateful. She would've felt cheap giving herself to such a man. And, though it was a contemptible thing to admit, he wanted her only for him. To not have been touched, defiled by others. He knew what that made him—a hypocrite of the highest order. But she was his, dammit!

Whoa... His? No, she wasn't his. What the hell was wrong with him?

'So why did you stop?' she asked faintly. 'That night. In the pool-house. Didn't I disappoint you too?'

Dante raked his palm over the hard ridges of his aching stomach. 'You think you disappointed me?'

Cristo, what would that have done to her confidence? Then, after him, Van Horn. 'No, *cara*. No. You were grieving, it was not right.'

Disappoint him? *Maledizione*, she couldn't be further from the truth.

He wanted her to be confident in her body. Not for him. Only for her. All that passion seemed to be restrained by vulnerability and a lack of self-confidence he had engendered. Well, he was damn well fixing it. Right now. Her purity was gone and the devil would dance in heaven before he allowed her only memory of this night to be one of pain.

Dante slowly backed her up against the glass wall, unravelling the sash on her gown, unwrapping her provocative body to his eyes, unveiling a plain white bra and matching panties—which drove him crazier than any G-string or crotchless slip he'd *ever* seen.

'Did it look like I was disappointed, *cara*? Does this,' he said, curving his hands around her small waist, delving lower to cup her lush, round cheeks and hauling her against his pelvis, 'does *this* feel like you don't turn me on?'

A little shiver. A little shake of her head.

'You are the *sexiest* woman alive. I am no virgin, Eva, and I can tell you right now I have never *ever* been so desperate to get inside someone as I am you, *capisci*?'

She nodded. Chest rising and falling. Soft skin spilling from her bra.

'I want this lethal, gorgeous body naked,' he said, voice thick and husky with want. 'It is a constant craving. Like a ticking time bomb, one touch to detonate, one thrust to explode. And I am going to watch you explode time and time again until you cannot think of what that useless bastard said to you. Only what I am doing to you. With my fingers, my mouth, my wicked tongue and my painfully hard…' Brushing up the side of her face, knowing it drove her wild, he whispered the word in her ear—the dirty variation he knew would flip her trigger—and he felt her stomach scrunch, her spine hit the glass.

Resting his brow against hers, he luxuriated in the heat seeping from her body, oozing into his. 'Do you pleasure yourself, Eva?'

He heard her audible gulp. Knew that was the only answer she was capable of.

One hand still holding her mind-blowing curvaceous derrière, Dante caught hold of her left hand, raised it to his mouth and nipped and sucked her ring finger from tip to base, watching her cheeks flush and her thick hazel lashes grow heavy.

As he twisted her hand this way and that, her yellow diamond caught fire and that possessiveness was back with a vengeance, pervading his chest until his ribs cracked at the thought of her taking it off to walk away, to leave him. *It's only because you're her first; it will wane. It must.* 'And do you wear my ring, Eva? Do you think of me while you touch?'

Body visibly seething with desire, she could barely breathe. 'Yes.'

He felt her knees give way and he thrust his thigh up between her legs to stop her fall. Within seconds, she was rocking against him. And, *Cristo*, he could feel her hot, wet heat at his thigh, scorching his skin.

The notion he may lose it flashed through his mind, yet he discarded it just as quickly. This time he'd take it slow. Replace every imperfect memory of earlier with a night she would never forget. The first time she deserved.

Eva gripped his shoulders, fingered his hair. 'I need…'

'What?' he said, licking across her bottom lip, kissing the corner of her full mouth. 'Tell me exactly what you need, what you want. I will give you everything you have ever desired of me.'

Chin dipping, Eva glanced at her bra. He caught her meaning instantly.

Why dislike being touched there? An inkling that it pertained to her mother slithered into his mind and his stomach fisted. But now was not the time. He would fix it. Later.

'So we take it one step at a time,' he said. 'First time we leave it on and I will touch you everywhere but your breasts. *Sì?*'

'You can do that?' she asked, her eyes flicking up to his, striking green pools connecting to his like powerful magnets.

'*Sì*. Of course.' It would take every scrap of self-control but he would do it. For her. And, just so she could relax, he admitted, 'You will soon discover I am bottom-half kind of guy, *cara*.'

'Oh. Yes. I think I've noticed.'

With a half smile designed to make her bones liquefy, he said, 'Trust me.' And swept feather-light kisses down her soft stomach, revelling in her sweet moans and the gooseflesh that arose on her almond skin. Then he delved into her panties, deeper into her wet folds, stroking, probing and swirling.

The urge to replace his fingers with his mouth, bury his tongue to taste her sweetness, coursed through him, making his mouth beg, his pulse quicken. So much so, he gripped her waist to keep her upright, ready to fall to his knees. And *devour*.

But, before he did, she fisted his hair, undulated atop his hand and pulled him down for a kiss. His kiss. Only his. And all he could think was: mine. Mine. Mine.

For one night only.

Eva belonged to him.

CHAPTER NINE

OVER AND OVER, Dante pushed her to the wicked edge of oblivion and tossed her into the deep, dark realms of ecstasy. Until she was boneless. A boneless quivering mass of thrumming desire. Until the sky was velvet black and the moon waxed in fullness.

Heart pounding, blood rushed through her veins as they finally, *finally* tumbled upon the bed, Eva cushioned atop piles of luxurious silk pillows, while Dante braced his weight on his forearms either side of her head, caging her with his long, hard, muscular body—a body vibrating with arousal, stretched to its very limits by his infinite patience.

Silver ribbons of light spun through the windows and her heart stumbled at the sight of her dark phantom hovering above her—colour slashing his cheekbones, eyes black with desire. And she couldn't resist because the man was a primal male fantasy come to life, so she ran her fingertips over his washboard abs, down the sweat-slicked super-sexy V of muscle on his pelvis and curled her fingers around his thick satiny length…

Dante sucked air between his teeth, jerked from her touch. 'No, *cara*.' And gently pulled her wrist away. 'Give me a minute. *Cristo*, I cannot think when you touch me.'

'Don't think. I want you now,' she said, smoothing her fingers round the tight curve of his rear, which she cupped and squeezed to lure him inside her. So very deep. Until she felt whole. Wanted. Desired. By him. Only him.

'Eva,' he growled, slashing his mouth over hers, one hand diving into her hair, the other roaming over her waist and hip with a covetous, mind-blowing touch.

A touch he withheld from her breasts. Breasts that ached with an inexplicable heavy need. So sensitive, she fought with the sudden desire to be free of the white fabric encasing, clutching. But if she tried, took it off, he would see. He would know. And he could *never* know. So she leashed the need—something she sensed in him too. Leaving her vaguely aware that they both held something back.

It was the rapacious predator in him. Dark. Perilous. That savage intensity that made her feel truly alive. Harnessed by the brutal power that was all Dante Vitale. So virile. So heart-stoppingly male.

Yet as soon as the void bubbled in her brain, it popped on a red-hot pinprick of rapture as he traced over her knee before slowly, seductively gliding up the inside of her thigh, stopping short of her wet curls. Wet from his mouth, where his tongue had lapped and kissed, tearing orgasm after orgasm from her shuddering body.

And, right now, she could taste that very essence, her blood already addicted, thirsting for more, and so she held him to her, tangling her tongue with his, drinking *them* in. Knowing. Her dreams hadn't come anywhere near close to the divine reality of him.

'Eva...Eva...' he murmured—making her heart throb—as he eased one hand under her bottom to lift, to tilt, so he could snuggle hard and tight in the apex of her thighs. And, *oh boy*, the sensation of his thick length pressing shot her straight back to that wicked edge and she undulated, grinding her pelvis into him.

'Slow, *cara*. Only pleasure,' he said, voice hoarse as his breathing escalated. 'You are so small inside.' His bronzed skin damp, big body trembling as if he feared hurting her.

'Take me… *Please.*' Just give me this. Memories to hold, to cherish, to remember.

As if she were made of the finest French lace, able to tear under the slightest of pressure, he eased the wide velvet tip of his erection inside her, so very gently. And her heart, *oh, God*, her heart ached. Ached so much she brushed the damp hair from his brow and stared into his dark eyes—watched them grow heavy, glaze out of focus with her every touch—as he finally took her. Because she didn't want to miss this moment. The one she'd been waiting for all her life. The connection so startlingly intense she felt tears clot her throat, prick the back of her eyes.

Panic seeped into her chest and in that moment she understood her craving for him to unleash. Because like this he posed more danger to her heart. He was almost making love to her. If she closed her eyes, she could pretend, dream as she used to so long ago, that this was her wedding night, *their* wedding night, and she'd saved herself for him. Only him. And such dreams did not belong in this bed. They were the dreams of a naive heart. A girlhood crush. Not the dreams of a woman who knew the limitations of her life. Knew the agony from loving another.

'*Cara*, tell me if you pain.' *Easy*, he entered her and her sheath tightened, pulled, sucking him in.

Her head pressed hard into the pillow and she arched sinuously. 'You feel *amazing*, Dante. So good. I want more. I want all of you.' *I always have. Your heart, your soul…* No. No! She didn't. Not any more. This was just sex, passion. Lust.

'Eva…' Pure animalistic, a groan, long and deep, came from the depths of his chest, calling to her, spurring self-preservation, refashioning it into recklessness, pulling him down for another kiss. A kiss to blow his mind, make him lose control. All heat and need and want as she writhed to take him deeper, curling her legs around his lean hips, hugging him closer.

'More.'

'*Cristo*,' he groaned, sinking in the last incredible inch until their bodies locked into place. Like two halves of a puzzle clicking together. And the relief, *oh*, the relief was unlike anything she'd ever known. It made her fall back into the mattress, nestle her face in his neck and just…breathe…in and out…breathe him in—all raw masculine power and dark desire.

Time stilled in a unique fragile trance as they lay that way, holding, clutching.

Dante murmured against the sensitive skin where

her neck met her shoulder, his every hot breath enticing a shiver. 'You feel like heaven, *cara mia*, you taste like heaven. You are mine, Eva. Mine.' All possessive domination.

Even knowing it made her a fool, she couldn't help but luxuriate in the vibrant violence behind his words.

'I'm yours.' And she was. For this moment. The most amazing of her life.

'Kiss me,' she begged. Because the man could rock her world with just a kiss and he growled into her mouth, before his lips stole her breath.

Flexing his hips, he began to move in and out of her—slowly at first, focused solely on her pleasure, kissing her face, sucking softly on her neck, smoothing his hand down her thigh, caressing her bottom.

'Do you have any idea what you do to me? Do you, Eva?' His dark accent hummed over her skin, notching the heat to danger levels, and she pulsed and clenched with the force of another climax, her lower abdomen now a spool spinning faster and faster, wrapping in luxurious velvet...

'Dante...' She kept breathing his name and each time she did his rhythm grew fiercer as if hearing her chant his name fed his fire. So for the first time in her life she danced beneath a warm deluge of female power.

'Speak to me,' she implored. 'I love it when you speak to me.' Feet flat to the bed, she pushed up into his hard strokes, moaning when he swivelled his hips to lick her sweet spot with the base of his shaft, sparks flying with the friction.

'Eva, *tesoro*, slow, slow,' he groaned huskily, voice pained, body vibrating as he grappled with the reins of his control.

Dancing closer to the flame, she bit the flesh of his bottom lip, threw his thrusts off tempo and wrung a deep feral groan from his chest.

'Dammit, Eva.' Grabbing her wrists, he pinned her to the bed as if he owned her. Eyes glittering with fire as he towered over her. 'So much passion,' he said, voice gruff. 'Never have I felt anything like you.' His big body flexed above her, muscles bunching as he ground against her. Slowly. Deliberately.

Electricity began to nip her skin, sizzle in the air…

Then, *boom*, it was hands everywhere they could reach, lips clashing, moans coalescing, control obliterated.

'Yesss…'

Dante's voice dropped to a low thrum as he drove

inside her in a hot, sensual rhythm, murmuring in his native tongue. A litany of thick Italian to maraud her senses. God, she wished she knew what he was saying because it sounded so wonderful, ignited all the colours in her heart, slamming her body past the point of no return.

'*Dante*...' A lightning crack of energy ripped through her core and she arched like a bow, shoulders digging into the downy pillows. Suspended. Captured on a sensually erotic plateau.

Dante's awed tone drifted from the other side. '*Cristo*, Eva,' as he stroked two blunt fingertips down her chin, swirled down the column of her throat, 'look at you. *Maledizione*, let go...' he demanded hoarsely. 'Let go, *cara*.' Lifting his torso just a touch, he rubbed her clit with the pad of his thumb rhythmically. 'Come for me, Eva. Come for me. *Now*.' And *whoosh*, the spool unravelled in hot, delicious waves of bliss, her entire body seizing in rapture while her world broke apart.

Suddenly fearful, a wild vulnerability quaked through her body until she shook—shook so hard she was petrified she'd never stop.

Anchoring, *needing* his strength, she wrapped her arms around him, vaguely aware she was murmuring in his ear, hoping he adored the sound of her voice when he came as much as she loved his.

Telling him how amazing he felt inside her, how hard she wanted him, how deep, only him. Only ever him.

'*Eva*,' he said, like a plea. So she held him tight, so tight to her.

His big body was racked as he was tossed into the heart of the storm, spilling heat, hips pumping long and hard in a mind-blowing rush. The shuddering fever-pitch engulfing her with gratification that she did this to him. Gave him pleasure. It made her feel wonderful. Deliciously happy.

Then her heart screamed, stay. *Stay with me. Please don't leave. Hold me in your arms. Just tonight.* The night she wanted never to end. But of course it had to. Reality would puncture the hazy dream until only memories lingered like wisps of bliss. The truth of her life would rise with the dawn. Depart on his jet. But not yet. Even if he stayed until she slept. It would be enough.

Storing every last second to her heart, Eva drifted down from the glorious heights like a shower of rainbow confetti—her body fluttering, the place between her legs beating out a soft tattoo of lingered pleasure, as they lay in each other's arms, lips moving over jaw and throat, nuzzling, soothing, calming.

Dante brushed down the side of her face—reverently, tenderly—at odds with the sudden hard edge of his voice. As if the man who'd just delivered her to ecstasy was no more than an illusion. A dream. 'Sleep, *cara mia*. I must work.'

'Okay,' she whispered on a slumberous sigh that feathered the aching wall of her throat as he gently unlocked their bodies, taking his glorious heat and strength with him. Leaving her cold. Empty. Bereft.

A heavy sensation that dragged the weight of her exhaustion and pulled her into the depths.

Until a thick curse burst from his lips and her eyes flew open. Connected with his. Then burned from the flames of fury she saw there.

Disgust twisted his lips, but it was the remorse hanging in the air that tore a seam up her midriff.

'Dante?' *Oh, no. No! Please, no regrets.*

Supple, agile, he lunged from the bed, throwing himself to his feet, anger crackling in every movement.

Standing like some bronzed god, he was totally, gloriously magnificent in his nakedness and she felt an astonishing twist of renewed heat–

'Are you protected?' he bit out. 'On the contraceptive Pill?'

And, with a deft push, she tumbled from heaven straight into hell.

* * *

Dante spun on a flaring blast of energy, spied his black silk lounge trousers and snatched them from the hardwood floor. Dragging them up the taut contours of his legs, he was vaguely aware that Eva did much the same at the opposite side of the room, snagging a white scrap from the back of a chaise, no doubt the closest thing to hand.

Swivelling to face her, he caught the white ripple of her linen sundress glissading down her sleek thighs, veiling skin that shimmied with pearlescent dew from an erotic fever the likes of which he'd never known.

Cristo, he'd always known she would be the death of him. Clearly, as soon as his angel hit the sheets her halo disintegrated. If he'd ever wondered if there was a creature who could unearth the dark passion that ran a black river beneath his skin, Eva was his answer.

Since when had he—Dante Vitale, the bastard heir—forgotten protection? Such loss of total control.

Since Eva.

Anger seeped into his brain like venom, swirling his vision in a black mist.

Cristo, one touch of that sinful body and he'd lost his mind. *Never* had he come so hard. Explosives being dangerous had been an ironic distortion. Detonation had obliterated every brain cell, and he doubted he would've sensed a tsunami thundering through the house, never mind the blatant lack of latex.

Weak. She made him weak. A condition he loathed. A condition that had just landed him in the dishonourable ranks of his father.

'Is it a safe time or…?' he asked, keeping his voice easy, modulated, despite the seething chasm opening in the pit of his stomach waiting to consume her answer.

Brow pinching with pain, she shook her head in tiny little jerks. 'It's probably the worst time.'

Horrified. She was horrified. Of course she was. The only thing she'd ever wanted from him was one night. Of sex.

Had his mother looked horrified when she'd suspected she was pregnant with him? So utterly mortified?

A look. A torture he could not physically bear.

Turning, he paced back and forth before bracing his hands, his entire weight, on the rounded lip of the dresser and bowed his head. Closed his eyes, trying to rid his mind of that look.

'Let's not jump the gun, okay? What are the chances?'

His famed forethought abandoned him. 'Of history repeating itself?' With their chemistry? 'Fairly damn high in my book.' It would be just his luck.

Then his conscience was a bloodying assault, one deft punch and kick after another. Cracking ribs, colouring his insides black and blue.

Not only had he stripped her of her innocence, he'd failed to protect her.

Maledizione! A possible child. One she didn't even want.

'History repeating itself?' she said faintly. 'What are you talking about?'

His insides writhed like a venomous snake pit.

Trudging in the mire of his parents' affair had never appealed to him—hell, he'd never given it a second thought—but there he stood, reliving his mother's drunken tales of woe and, before he knew it, the words were hissing from his mouth.

'My father took my mother's innocence,' he bit out. 'Slaked his lust. Used her up and tossed her out. Ruined her reputation by walking away when she was pregnant with me.' A heinous dishonour Dante had no intention of repeating.

'Oh, Dante, your mum must've been so scared, left alone like that.'

Head jerking upright, he watched his brow crease in the dresser mirror.

Not once had he thought about how it had affected his mother. Had she been scared? Knowing she'd had no choice but to bring him up alone? Had the wait been terrifying, just to find out? Alone.

He doubted it. But what was more telling was that Eva immediately empathised.

Dante spun on his heel to search her beautiful face.

Pale. So pale. A stark contrast to her lips, bruised crimson from the crush of his mouth. Was she scared? Was *that* the look on her face?

Cristo, of course she was. What was wrong with him? He needed a bloody instruction manual to read her.

'But that doesn't mean history will repeat itself,' she said softly. Was she was trying to make *him* feel better? 'I'm not your mum and you're not your dad.'

Too right he wasn't. And no, Eva wasn't like his mother. Old Eva had wanted children, hadn't she? Problem was, he wasn't sure which Eva he was looking at from one moment to the next.

Regardless, he had no intention of allowing her to worry alone. This was his fault and he was fixing it.

'You will stay here until we know, *capisci*?' he said fiercely. Maybe a little too harshly if the stunned arch of her blonde brows was anything to go by. 'If you are…'

Dante waited for the barbed wire to wrap around his guts at the thought of another marriage. So why the hell relief was a warm river rushing through his system he'd never know. *Because she will belong to you. No one else can touch her.*

Then, before he could even attempt to stem the flood, the fathomless depths of Natalia's betrayal sucked him down into the dregs. Where, instead of Natalia lying on the sheepskin rug in front of his hearth, entwined with another, it was Eva. Eva telling him he was cold, frozen to the core. Eva finding comfort in the arms of another while he was continually away on Vitale business. And where he'd felt naught but fury at Natalia's deceit, the mere thought of finding Eva with another…

A monstrous hand gripped his stomach and twisted tight. Black poison oozed through his veins, flooding his mind with corrupted toxic visions and he scrambled for the antidote.

Rules. His rules. He'd tie her up in a marriage contract so tight she wouldn't dare wriggle free by deceit or adultery. One false move and he'd take his child to the far side of the earth.

This time he'd have total control.

The black mist cleared from his vision and he focused back on Eva. Mouth working around a retort at his indelicate demand that she stay, her beautiful dainty hand fluttering around the dip of her waist and circling the linen shrouding her stomach.

Right then, the most spectacular sensation inflated his chest.

Hope. Strong. Unwavering.

Eva would carry the Vitale heir. Finally he'd have a son to pass on the legacy he'd fought so long and hard for.

'Dante, you can't be serious. I can't stay here. I have to work.'

Commanding every emotion in his body to shut down with ruthless efficiency, Dante rolled his shoulders and flexed his neck.

Knowing. His powers of persuasion were unequalled.

So he would tempt. Lure. And she *would* surrender.

'I am deadly serious, Eva. Because if you are, we will marry right here on the island and no one will ever suspect.'

So, until they knew for sure, he wasn't letting Eva out of his sight.

CHAPTER TEN

BRAIN IN LOCK-FUNCTION, it took Eva a good few seconds for the cogs to turn. '*What*?'

Marry? Her and *Dante*?

'Forget jumping the gun, you've pulled the trigger.' Of course he had. He was being Dante. Powering forward, two steps ahead of time. As if he could see into the future and wanted to control it *now*. 'Let's just wait and see. If I am p…pregnant we'll discuss the future then. Okay?'

Standing at the opposite side of the bed, washed in the silvery light of the moon, he looked like some Prince of Darkness. Staring at her. With a sinful smile that was a dangerous mix of cold-blooded ruthlessness and annihilating charm, eliciting an ominous sense of déjà vu.

Her spine smacked against the panoramic window with no idea how she'd retreated ten feet and still her eyes devoured him.

'And will you please put some clothes on.' Already the hot splash of desire was swirling in her midriff. Hungry. She craved him. Didn't her body realise they were in enough trouble as it was?

A ghost of a killer *knowing* smile hovered around his lips and she spun on her bare feet, gripped the door lever, wrenched the glass panel wide and burst into the midnight air—thick with tropical heat and just as cloying.

Marry Dante? *Oh, boy.*

Heavens above, her mind was still trying to wrap itself around the possibility of a baby.

So Eva was *not* envisioning a picturesque little church, crawling with ivy and pink roses washed in morning sunlight. And she most certainly was *not* designing an A-line gown with elbow-length sleeves layered with floating lace appliqué. She was not!

Pins stabbed the backs of her eyes and Eva scrunched them shut. 'I promise you, Dante. Whatever happens, you don't want to marry me. I'm a living nightmare.'

'I know this, *cara*,' he said dryly. 'But do not feel too badly. It makes life…interesting.'

A reluctant smile played about her lips. One that she crushed a wrenching heartbeat later. 'Interesting isn't always good.'

The soothing sound of cool waves lapping at the shore was like music to her ears and she veered towards the spiral staircase at the far end of her veranda like some kind of frantic Cinderella. Running before the clock struck twelve and Dante discovered the reality of her life.

'Eva!'

'Not now, Dante.'

Down and around she went, the cold metal balustrade biting into her palm, her bare soles pad-pad-padding down the smooth, blissfully chilled tiles.

'Eva, what the hell are you running from?'

My life. The truth. Because any minute now he would catch up with her and if she ran he would never know. Finn would never know. No more pain for her family. Not as long as she drew breath.

At the sound of his heavy footfall she jumped off the bottom rung and sank into the white icing-sugar sand, tinted pale silver from the stark glare of moonlight.

'I just want to be by myself. Okay?'

'No. It is not okay,' he ground out.

Catching up with her halfway to the water's edge, he curled his warm fingers around the soft flesh of her upper arm and tugged her to face him.

'I want your vow you will stay and if you're pregnant we will marry.'

'I can't stay. I have two weddings on Christmas

Eve. Which leads me on to my second point. *I* don't want to get married. To anyone. *Ever.*'

Darkness descended as if the moon had been usurped by the blackest of clouds and she shivered wildly. There was something almost terrifying in his splintering gaze.

'Why?' he ground out with sarcastic bite. 'Because, let me tell you, you make no sense, Eva. Why does an innocent, who lives and breathes romance, not *do* devotion?'

The cynicism contorting his face was like pouring fuel on the petrol of her ire and sparked a retaliation that, quite frankly, had been a long time coming. The words exploded from her mouth without a single thought. 'Because I've seen enough heartbreak and pain to last me ten lifetimes. So I'm not willing to devote my life to a man who believes the word monogamous equates to one woman in every city. When I grew up with one who thought nothing of scratching his itch while his wife suffered and his children rotted!'

Heart threatening to burst from her heaving chest, Eva watched understanding relax his tight features. Unfurl his fists.

'*Cristo*, why didn't I see this?' Tipping his head back, he glared at the starlit sky and blew out a ragged breath. 'Eva, *cara*, not all men are weak.'

Chin lowering, he locked on to her eyes and jammed his thumb in his chest. 'I am *not* your father.'

'Weak?' she said, wincing at the crack in her voice. 'That's what people call adultery and desertion now? A weakness?'

'*Sì*. It is a weak man who leaves his wife and children when times are hard.'

Eva slammed her hands on her hips. 'Or maybe it's a man who believes one woman equates to eternal boredom. Let's face it, you have just as much staying power. Finn too.'

Nostrils flaring, she watched his wide chest swell. 'You know nothing of my staying power, Eva. Do not judge me without a fair hearing. I have never lied about my intentions or cheated on another. If you knew—'

Blinking, she pondered the pain marring his staggeringly beautiful face. 'Knew what?'

'I would *never* do such a thing to you.'

No one could dismiss the sincerity blazing in his fierce gaze and she wanted to believe him. Desperately. But the doubts lingered on. Maybe it was because she was *nothing* like his other women. Or maybe she realised he would soon tire of a wife who couldn't even make love with her bra off. How long would his patience last then? What if she lost her breasts altogether? Would he want her then? Of course he wouldn't. Not when he could have any woman in the world.

'We would always have truth, you and I. Always honesty. Without messy emotions overruling common sense.'

Messy emotions? Wasn't that just a typical Dante remark?

'I appreciate what you're saying, I do. But marriage is not the answer.' She refused to ensnare him in her life.

'Let me make one thing very clear, Eva.' Darkness, like demon shadows creeping over a soul, clouded his eyes with...*pain*? 'No son of mine will question his existence, no son of mine will be without his father's name.'

Eva blinked, his seething dominance shuttering in and out of view. Such normal words, yet the agony, the violence behind them.

Suddenly, the penny dropped. His father had never acknowledged him. Or at least until he'd had no choice. When his mother had died? Oh, God, what must that have been like for him? No wonder he was jumping ahead of time. Picturing the worst. *History repeating itself.*

Eva reached up. 'I promise you, *if* I am pregnant, he or *she* can still have your name. I swear—'

He jerked from her touch and her hand plummeted to her side. 'Forgive me if I do not trust your promises, *cara*. There is more to consider here than your obstinacy. We have business reputations to protect. Finn to consider. The happiness and well-being of a child. We *will* marry.'

Eva closed her eyes. He was right. She knew it. If they didn't marry, Dante would look all kinds of a louse and, as for her... *Ohh,* boy. She could see the headlines now: Diva Up The Duff! Who's The Father? Finn would murder Dante with his bare hands. In truth their child would need him. He was right. *If* she was pregnant, they would have to marry.

'Yes. Okay. If. If. Don't forget the *if.* Oh, God, this is awful.' Dante would be stuck with her for life. Or at least until she fell sick. How was she supposed to tell him? That one of his one-night-wonders might turn out to be his worst nightmare.

Stomach churning violently, she pushed the flat of her palm against her belly-button and breathed deep. How could the most amazing night of her life go so horribly wrong?

'Is marriage to me so distasteful, Eva?' There it was again. A sharp edge of something close to a sting. Oh, he tried to hide it, lighten it with a wry tone, but it was there, she knew. As if she'd offended him. 'Or is being tied down with my child so distasteful?'

'No,' she insisted, forking her fingers through her hair, pulling to redirect the pain shredding her heart. 'No!'

'Then speak to me, *cara*,' he said, frustration lacing his accent. 'You make no sense. *Maledizione*! One minute I am at the Gala, staring at the Diva, and tonight I am lying in bed with Eva. Beautiful young Eva, who told me she wanted three children. Two boys and a girl.'

Every muscle in her body froze. 'I...I told you that?' Grateful for the dark night sky, she felt heat flush up her cheeks at the untimely reminder of one of her more excruciatingly gauche attempts at figuring him out.

'*Sì*,' he said, unfazed.

A sharp, sweet ache pierced her chest. The kind where if she were alone she would be gasping for air, rocking to make the pain abate. So she had no idea how she found the strength to stand tall, to even speak. 'That Eva doesn't...' Exist any more. 'She's...she's...' Gone. Grew up in the real world.

Turning her back on him, knowing she was being a coward for doing so, she faced the lapping froth of the incoming tide, stared at calm waters rippled with the silver reflection of the moon. 'I decided a long time ago that life isn't for me.' *Tell him, tell him—it's the only way to change his mind.* 'Because there's a good chance, a *high* chance, I might get sick. Like my mother…and my grandmother.'

The clammy air grew thicker still, swirling around her with a tension she couldn't grasp. Then his voice came to her, dark as the sky above, smooth as the richest velvet, touched with warm understanding. 'Ah, Eva, finally I see you.'

Crushing her lips together, she squeezed her eyes shut and breathed in a deep shuddering breath, inhaling the fresh salty tang of the sea.

'Does Finn know this?' he asked.

'No. I don't want him worrying. He didn't take Mum being sick so well.' With one hand she pulled her hair over one shoulder and rubbed a silky strand between her fingertips. 'So *please* don't tell him.'

More silence. And still she couldn't turn. Look at him. For fear of what she might see. Pity? Or maybe remorse. For surely it was dawning on him that he might be stuck with a wife who waited for the axe to fall.

Heat. Scorching heat seeped into her back. As if he'd moved closer and she could feel the almighty strength he exuded rolling off his body in pulsating waves. Yet he didn't touch. Not once. Even as her heart begged him to take her in the lashing strength of his arms and tell her everything would be okay. Even as she hated that weakness. That need. Knew it was far safer not to need a living soul.

'Look at me, *cara*.'

She couldn't—she couldn't. 'Dante—' her voice was thick, clotted with tears, trembling '—I'm so sorry. I'm just as much to blame. I should have thought of protection myself.' *Oh, God.* She should *never* have succumbed to the temptation of him. 'I never want to put a child through what I went through.'

The touch of his warm fingers curling over the balls of her shoulders made her flinch. 'Look at me!' he demanded with a quiet, savage intensity, spinning her around to face him.

'I am not your father, Eva. I am not a weak man. I will be there for our child. I swear it.' Sincerity scored his face. 'I am strong enough and powerful enough to shield him from every storm and I will *never* let you down. You believe me, *Sì*?'

Eva nodded slowly, dazed by the ferocity of his declaration.

'Say it, Eva!'

Words burst from her lips. 'I believe you.' She did. Absolutely.

In that moment Eva had never wanted to touch him more. To kiss, to ease the stark pain haunting every angle of his riveting bone-structure.

And why was he looking at her in that way? As if he was about implode with the emotions pummelling his body. She'd do anything to know what he was thinking. Anything. Was he regretting every second of this night?

He reached up and brushed a damp tendril of hair from her brow before his gorgeous face came closer, closer. While her hopeful heart missed a beat waiting for his kiss. *Yes, please—kiss me, make love to me, show me you still want me, make me forget.*

Warm lips touched her brow. Tender. Amiable. The notion that this was the first kiss she'd ever hated spread through her mind like a blood-red stain. 'Stay until we know, *cara.*'

'I can't. The boutique is in enough trouble as it is and I have orders to go out. Dresses to finish.'

Frustration oozed out of his taut frame as he pulled back. As if he didn't want to let her out of his sight. Eva knew better.

All the times she'd dreamed of marrying Dante, his proposal was never sewn by the threads of honour. All the times she'd secretly dreamed of having his baby—all thick, dark, yummy hair and amazing deep umber eyes—it was never trapping him by the treacherous hands of fate. But back then she'd been living in fairy tales. But this? This was reality.

Tipping her head skyward, she gazed at the diamante-studded brilliance. Focused on the biggest, brightest star. *I've messed up big style this time, Mum. I just couldn't help myself. He's my weakness. But you always knew that, right?*

Thousands of pinpricks stabbed her clogged throat. A solitary tear escaped, trickled down the side of her face.

'Ah, Eva...' he said, sweeping her into his arms bride-style and enveloping her in his white-hot heat.

Weaving her arms around his shoulders, she buried her face in his neck as he carried her into the house. And the lashing strength of his arms was the final dent in her armour. Or maybe it was the way he peeled the white sundress from her body and made love to her with a slow, seductive, exquisite intensity she was powerless against. He made her forget, he made her feel alive, so gloriously alive. So by the time she shattered in his arms he had her oath to stay one more day.

One more day in paradise.

CHAPTER ELEVEN

Dante leaned against the door-jamb of his kitchen, crossed his arms over his naked chest and contemplated the pitfalls of an idyllic mansion while the frantic pounding of his heart slowed.

There she was.

Rooting through the cupboards, her caramel tresses rippled down her back and his eyes devoured her half-dressed state, her habitual bra smothered by a white silk vest and matching shorts laced with baby-pink ribbons.

Eva St George. Soon-to-be Eva Vitale if his hunch proved correct.

After receiving the marriage contracts through from London, he'd gone to check on her before returning to his own suite—one cold bed, blood freezing in his veins.

Although in hindsight he should've known where he'd find her. How many times had he caught her wandering the St George kitchen in the dead of night, hips swaying in a natural hypnotic rhythm, sensuality drenching her glorious body in a light sheen as she prowled to satisfy her sweet tooth.

So young. Happy. Carefree.

An astonishing contrast to the heartbreaking vulnerability he'd been faced with on the beach. A woman who virtually hid from the world. All sass and obstinacy gone. Replaced by a fragility so un-Eva-like he'd worn a dagger in his gut ever since.

An off-key humming invaded his thoughts and he focused back on Eva, now on her tippy-toes, stretching sinuously to reach the top shelf. 'A-ha!'

Dante smiled knowingly and eased back against the door-jamb to drink her in. Quench his thirst.

Pulse flipping into high gear, he watched her twist the lid from *his* jar of chocolate spread and delve deep with a long-handled café spoon. With a swirl of her hand, she plucked it free and popped the glob of chocolate between her pink lips.

Eyes closed, Eva moaned in sheer ecstasy.

That was it. Lust—white and hot—poured down his spine, pooling in his groin, and he growled long and low.

Time slowed as she caught sight of him, jumped nigh on a foot in the air and let go of the jar.

Dante jolted forward as the thick glass smacked the travertine with a dull crack, the splatter of rich chocolate and hazardous shards inches away from her bare feet.

Eva slammed her hand over her left breast, 'Oh, my God—you gave me the shock of my life, you idiot!'

Willing his heart to calm, his gaze jerked up from her perfect little feet. 'Did it satisfy your craving, *cara*?'

Cheeks pinking, she gave her head a little shake. 'No, not really.'

Dante lips curved in a half smile. 'I know exactly what will.'

'You do?'

'*Sì.*' He closed the space between them, coming to a stop at the outer edges of the jar disaster. Holding out his arms, he beckoned her with a flick of his curled hand. 'Come to me.'

His guts took a deft kick when she hesitated, those mesmerising eyes wary, guard up.

Heart thudding, he counted four beats before her chest swelled on a loaded inhalation and she leaned forward, holding out her arms.

Dante lifted her clean off the floor, swivelled and plonked her on the black granite island in the centre of the vast space.

'Do you have a brush so I can clean up?' she asked.

'Stay there.'

'It's a good job you have flip-flops on.'

He didn't bother telling her he'd learned long ago not to walk anywhere without shoes. Paved streets in the dead of night when his mother was entertaining had been sole-splittingly hazardous.

Within five minutes he'd cleared the debris and opened one of the wide cases lining the kitchen with a tug of the lever handle.

Kerthunk went the door, with a suction sound that brought a sexy-as-hell curve to her lips. 'Freezer.'

'And what do you think,' he said, 'I could tempt you with in here, *Tesoro*?'

Hands either side of her hips, she launched off the bench and shot to his side.

'Please tell me you have macadamia nut or…or chocolate cookies…or—' Trailing off, her brow furrowed as she looked up at him, sussing him out with eyes as warm as the rarest emerald. *Affection*? No, he must be wrong. *You're as cold and dark as your father, Dante. How can anyone love you?*

'Dante, did you hear me?'

He breathed through the twist in his guts. 'Sorry, *cara.* Say again?'

'Is your favourite still Tiramisu?'

'Naturally,' he said, grabbing all three, relishing the icy bite on his palms. 'Where would you like to feast?'

'Outside. My balcony. I have the most delicious view.'

'I guarantee the mosquitoes will find you just as tasty, *tesoro*.'

'Who cares? I feel like living dangerously.' Words so lightly voiced, yet he could sense an underlying meaning behind them. And for the hundredth time he asked himself how the weight of her health risk had affected her. For clearly she bore it alone.

Cristo, his soul ached for her.

Twenty minutes later they were ensconced on a soft-cushioned swing seat, the sound of the waves lapping, the palms swishing in the breeze, dawn hovering on the horizon, heaped spoons in hand.

Lips cold, his tongue laced with coffee creaminess, his apparent genius was trying to figure out a way to approach the bra subject when she coughed out a laugh—

'Hey, do you remember the night I persuaded you and Finn to drive me to a twenty-four-hour store for ice cream?'

Like a vault opening wide, Dante allowed the memories to slither through the cracks of his mind. Eva, all huge green eyes peering up at him from between thick, gorgeous hazel lashes, begging him and Finn to drive her.

'It was a disaster,' she went on. 'Finn got pulled for speeding, managed to dodge three points by promising Dad would sing at the policeman's wedding—'

The tension in his midsection eased with a smile. '*Sì*, I remember.' As if it were yesterday.

'It took us hours to find this store and what happens?'

'No ice cream,' he said.

'I was devastated. Then Finn scored with the shop girl and you were…' she swallowed '…stuck with me.' Was it his imagination or did she literally choke on the word *stuck*? 'Boy, were you furious. Then again, you always were. People used to say Finn was day and you were night. I saw you as more of a thunderstorm. Dark and ominous. So angry.'

If he'd ever harboured the notion that Eva might think differently from his mother, that statement quashed it in a nanosecond.

'I did buy you a box of chocolates, *cara*, so the night was not a complete washout.'

'Yes, you did. I can't believe you remember that.'

The sensation of her stunned eyes searing over his face made him turn. 'What?'

'Nothing,' she whispered, shaking her head, attention back to the deep tub.

Maybe it was the hot crackle in the air, maybe it was the tension pulling taut. Whatever it was, Dante scooped another spoonful of Tiramisu and got back to topic. 'Did your father ever sing at that wedding?'

Lapping the base of the spoon with the flat of her pink tongue, she smiled. 'Yes, I think he did. I think Mum made him.' Her brow pleated. 'I can hear her now: *Nicky baby, you have to, Finn promised*. The look on my dad's face.' Spoon hovering in mid-air, her lips flattened as she gazed out to the ocean, unseeing. 'Pure indulgence. I forgot how he used to look at her.'

'Maybe you buried the good memories, *cara*.' In a vault. 'Buried under a weightier memory of his betrayal.'

'Yes,' she said, nodding, still staring out to sea. 'So many broken promises. So many lies. Even I lied to her beautiful pale face and every time my heart broke a little more. I burned newspapers so she wouldn't see photographs of his women. Told her he was on tour. Told her *anything* to stop her heart from breaking while she was in pain. She'd given him her heart and he betrayed her—he betrayed us all when we needed him so desperately and I'll never forgive him or myself.' Her voice cracked, making his stomach tighten. 'I should never have lied to her, Dante. Wherever she is, I just hope she forgives me.'

Cristo, little wonder she hated lies. Couldn't even speak them without blushing furiously. No doubt in remorse. How hard this past week must have been for her. Living and breathing untruths.

'I am sure of it, *cara*. Your mother will know you did it out of love.'

Eyes glossed with grief, her gaze sought his. 'You think so?'

Dante reached over and brushed the hair from her brow, stroked down her delicate jaw. 'I know so.'

When she nuzzled into his hand he couldn't help himself. He leaned over and kissed the pleat from her brow. 'He let her down. He let you all down. But not through lack of love. He is not a strong man, Eva. Maybe it hurt him too much to see her that way. In so much pain.'

The thought of Eva in pain…

Maledizione, when she'd told him. His insides had quaked with so much emotion he'd feared eruption but she wanted, *needed* his strength. So she would have it. Always.

'It hurt me too,' she said. 'But did I leave?'

'You are stronger than him. You handled your pain, your grief in different ways. You submerged yourself in the party scene. Perfect oblivion. Surrounded by people who couldn't hurt you. Maybe that's why you tried to sleep with Van Horn. You told me yourself you felt nothing, so there was no risk to your heart.'

Eyes wide, she blinked up at him. 'You're right, I did. I don't even see those people any more.'

'I remember so many things about your home. The love. Laughter.' The claw of longing down his chest, one he stuffed down into the depths, knowing that life was not possible for him. 'Keep the good memories in your heart, *cara.*'

Dante had no good memories of his childhood. He didn't want that for her.

'What do you remember about your home?' she asked warily.

The pot crumpled in his hand, jaw locking tight while he pondered brushing her off. *Cristo*, was the woman telepathic? Now he remembered why he didn't talk!

He didn't want pity from her soft heart. But nor did he want her to back off from him.

Clearing his throat, he focused on the hazy line where the sea met the oncoming dawn in a soft wash of pink. 'I remember nothing more than veering mood swings and broken vodka bottles, *cara*.'

Quiet descended and his fingers bleached white around the handle of his spoon, body braced for the onslaught of pity.

'Oh. No wonder you snatched that wine bottle off me at my eighteenth birthday party.' She nudged him lightly with her arm. 'Your mum and my dad would've made a great pair.'

Then. Then he remembered exactly who he was talking to. Eva. Always thinking of others before herself. With a remarkable flair for knowing exactly how and when to lighten the mood.

He couldn't help but return her small, knowing sassy smile. 'A better choice than my father,' he said. 'He ruined her.' Why had he never seen that before? When he knew Primo Vitale could strip self-respect with one acidic glance.

'Maybe that's where she buried her pain. In the bottom of a bottle,' Eva said, her brow a deep V. 'Do you think that's why my dad's drinking is worse than ever?'

'I imagine he is not very proud of himself, *tesoro*. He has to live with such guilt. I noticed at the Gala he can barely look at you. He is ashamed.'

Her face scrunched in a pretty confusion. 'You're right. Here I'm having trouble forgiving him and he has to live with guilt every day. Oh, Dante, I wish I could help him.'

'Already you have done so much for him, *cara*.' For a long moment he thought of his mother's tears. The gluttony of men, the binges. How furious and frustrated Dante had become that no matter what he said or did, he hadn't been able to help her. Nothing he'd done was good enough. 'He needs to find his own peace.'

It wasn't until he felt Eva's fingertips dust the back of his hand that he realised his entire body had seized. Their eyes caught...held. With a warmth, a connection he couldn't grasp. One that shifted to a sensual bent to thicken the air. And Eva's gaze dropped to his mouth as she shifted on her hip to face him. Her bare thigh nudging his. The hot friction spiking his pulse.

'Can I try your Tiramisu?'

Dante licked the creamy dribble from the base of the spoon and raised it to her open mouth, the sight of which set fire to his veins. Her lush lips closed around the silver and Dante watched a drop-let drizzle down the handle and plop upon the full curve of her left breast.

Evading the urge to lean forward and lick the sweetness from her skin, he wiped the glob with his thumb, raised it to her lips and watched her take the thick pad into her mouth to lick and suck as her pupils dilated.

Heat, swift and savage, flooded his veins, pooled at the base of his spine until his groin throbbed viciously. And the temptation to haul her in his lap and plunge into her hard and fast made his stomach quake. But her guard was low and this was his chance.

Fighting, fighting for control, he smudged his thumb over her full bottom lip…trailed it down the elegant sweep of her neck and slid a finger underneath one pure white bra strap. 'Do you ever take it off?'

'Sure I do,' she said, tucking a long caramel lock around her ear with an unsteady hand. 'In the shower.'

'Tell me why. Why dislike something so beautiful?'

'You mean apart from the fact they're big enough to fill a billboard and create carnage in Piccadilly Circus?'

Dante took the hit, remembering his quip at the Gala. *Cristo*, he'd been furious with her for doing it. But clearly, 'It bothered you.'

'Of course it bothered me. But I did it as a favour to Breast Cancer United. Then, after the pile-up, the hype was just humiliating. But I don't regret it. Apparently that ad raised millions in sponsors.'

'*Sì*. I am not surprised.' The thought of half the western world staring at seventy per cent of her breasts made the blood freeze in his veins. 'But I think this is only half the truth.' He knew it was. But he needed her to say it. To tell him. To trust him.

'Honestly? I think it started with my mother. I remember certain things so vividly. Her operations, when she lost them. I'm not sure how to explain, but...I kept putting myself in her shoes. Some days I could almost feel her pain.'

'Ah, Eva, you were so close to her, I am not surprised, *cara*.'

'It made me wish I wasn't a woman. And when...' The smooth column of her throat convulsed as she ditched the carton on the table beside her before she turned back to him. 'I've never spoken about this before, but I guess it's only right that you know.'

Unease swirled behind his ribs—or was it undiluted dread?—and he pushed his spine into the soft padded back. Waiting.

'A couple of years ago, I had a scare. I found a small lump. What with all the specialists and the tests and the biopsies and—'

'Whoa,' he said, holding up one hand while he flung his empty tub to the floor, arms aching to wrap her in his body. Except he doubted he would let go. Ever.

Strength—he needed to keep strong for her. 'You were *alone*?'

'Sure. I didn't *need* anyone.' Her slender throat convulsed. 'Turns out it was benign, so just a scare, that's all.'

Just?

Cristo, she must have been petrified. He could barely breathe thinking about it. And, knowing Eva, she'd have gone alone to protect Finn. To protect them all!

'Anyway, the long and short of it is—' she continued with bravado that belied the nervous flutter of her expressive hands '—I don't like them being touched and this…' she curled her fingers around the top edge of the lace cupping her left breast and tugged to reveal a white scar line about an inch long—a giant fist gripped his heart '…reminds me. So I always wear a bra and I suppose you could say it's become a habit that I can't shake. But, more recently, what with the fake kissing and the…sex… even when you look at me a certain way they feel different and I want you to touch me there, but it's hard for me to let go. Relax.'

Dante set his jaw hard enough to crack a molar. Specialists. Tests. Biopsies. 'So whenever you have been touched there, it has been impersonal, intrusive. Cold.' He swallowed. Around a boulder. 'Painful?'

Suddenly, he was staring at the top of her head as she watched her fingertips stroke the hem of her shorts. 'A little.'

He closed his eyes for a beat. Her feelings made sense. If she'd never experienced any pleasure from them, why would she feel any different?

A vision popped into his mind, a place he'd never taken another living soul. 'Have you brought a bikini with you?' he asked.

Blinking, her face scrunched in confusion at the swift change in conversation. 'Y-y-yes.'

'Good. I want to show you something. Here comes the dawn—get ready and I'll meet you downstairs in thirty minutes.'

'We're going somewhere? But don't you have to work?'

Dante switched off the incessant voices in his head. Yes, Vitale would always come first, but he hadn't had one day off in fifteen years, so he was sure he could spare her one day for this. 'Not today.'

A beautiful smile curved her lips and he was filled with the inexplicable urge to keep it there.

'Come with me, Eva. *Per favore*. Let's have some fun, *cara mia*.' When was the last time she did that? When was the last time she shed the weight of an unknown future?

'Always, your mother smiled, Eva. Smiled and said, "Life is not about waiting for the storm to pass. It's about learning to dance in the rain."'

CHAPTER TWELVE

LIFE IS NOT about waiting for the storm to pass. It's about learning to dance in the rain.

For the first time in years, Eva wanted to dance. Because Dante Vitale had actually taken a day off work. It boggled the mind. There was not one phone in this canoe. Although she doubted there was even room for one. Narrow and precarious didn't begin to cover it.

But the distinct lack of cellphones wasn't the reason a giddy swirl of exhilaration and anticipation hummed through her veins. Nope. It was because she was happy. *Keep the good memories in your heart, cara.* Just reliving the good times gave her a sense of peace she hadn't felt in years. So alive, she wanted to have fun. Do crazy things.

Like allowing herself to imagine, after years of denying herself the luxury. To nurture the notion that there could be a life flickering inside her. To think about marrying Dante. Having him always.

She wouldn't be alone any more. She didn't *want* to be alone any more.

After they'd made love last night, he'd kept touching her tummy as if he was envisaging. Already utterly convinced. And the gorgeous man had her doing the same. Dreaming up names and designing a christening gown. It was just absurd. Surreal. More than a little scary. Because she'd mooned over such things before. Could remember the bone-crushing pain of falling from magical clouds of happy ever after. *So don't expect more from him than he can give...*

'Love is for the weak and needy and I am neither.'

She just had to remember what they shared was passion. Lust that, when sated, he left to work or slip between his own cool sheets. In truth, making love was the only time she felt the power of his emotions. So, like an addict, she craved another fix. A higher dose of his lethal sexual dominance. Resistance was futile and she hated herself for the weakness.

Still, he'd taken a day off work for *her* and she wasn't wasting a minute.

Dante powered the oars from behind and the canoe sliced through the water, heading for a towering rock face. On approach, Eva could see the rock open up into a jagged split and streams of excitement washed down her chest, percolating inside her as the split swallowed them whole, plunging them into darkness.

'You still with me?' he asked.

'Absolutely. I love the dark.'

'You will not like it so much when your head collides with a stalactite, *tesoro*,' he said sardonically. Then his loud command, 'Lights,' echoed around her and the enormous cavern illuminated in a soft white glow, the lights flaring from the bottom of the lake.

Eyes adjusting, she inhaled sharply. 'Oh, *wow*! It's like something out of a fantasy. And those,' she said, pointing at the elongated straw-like formations hanging from the ceiling, 'look like crystals.' Huge rare chandeliers. Millions of years in the making. 'And the water,' she said, 'it's like a clear azure lake.'

'Duck.'

'Really? In here?'

Dante burst out laughing, the sound rich and throaty, drenched in masculinity, sending hundreds of tiny tremors through her core. *Wow*. She'd never heard him laugh before.

His laugh went on even as he pushed her head

down between her splayed legs. 'Quit, Eva, unless you really want this boat to go over.'

'*Boat*? You call this a boat?'

'Right, that's it. You asked for this.'

Before she knew what he was about, he leaned over, rocked once…twice and *splash*, over they went, headlong into the water. Water so warm her bones dissolved and she went lax, in no hurry to resurface.

Then the hot hands of the devil himself curled around her waist, gripping—protective, possessive, lifting….until the air smacked her face as she broke the surface.

Gasping, she rubbed the water from her eyes. 'You're a bad boy, Vitale.'

'Enjoying yourself down there?' Voice raspy, he exhaled raggedly and that touch of concern sprang her eyes wide.

Brow lined, Dante searched her face, stared at the pulse she could feel fluttering at the base of her throat. Then he squeezed her waist for one, two, three beats of her swelling heart.

It was silly, pointless, but Eva began to search right back. Looking for something, anything that told her he truly cared. About *her*. Because there were so many little things that could mean something but she'd been here before, hadn't she? Misread every sign, every loaded glance. Searching. Hoping for more. Only to be crushed beyond repair. Ache until she could barely breathe. *So stop looking, Eva!*

Suddenly he blinked and spun her around until her back crushed into his front and thought vanished.

'See over there,' he said, pointing to a sliver in the rock wall where natural daylight peeped into the cavernous space.

'I see it.'

'That's your reward if you do everything I ask of you in the next twenty minutes. I will show you heaven on earth.'

A seam of unease tore up her spine while ruffles of exquisite elation spun up her midriff. 'Everything you ask?'

'*Everything* I ask. I swear I will not hurt you and if at any time you wish me to stop, you have only to say the word.'

'What word?' she asked breathlessly.

Flicking her earlobe with his nose, he whispered in her ear and her eyelids shuttered.

'And you'll show me heaven?'

'I'll show you more than heaven, *cara*.'

No thought, no hesitation. In truth, she'd never felt so alive. 'I'll do it.'

Dante exhaled harshly, his breath fanning her nape as he curled his arm around her waist and yanked her tight against him. Her bottom nudged his groin and if she'd been in any doubt as to what was on his mind, the hard length of his arousal quashed it with stunning effect.

With her back to his front, he moved them through the water until they reached a jagged lip. 'Up.' He lifted her clean out of the water and she stumbled forward a step. 'Don't turn around.'

So Eva waited. For his touch, for his command. Her heart a *bump, bump,* thumping beat, her hands trembling.

Slosh—she heard him leap from the water. 'Close your eyes,' and he came flush against her once more, steering her pathway with his hard body.

Jerkily they came to a stop and she was smacked with so many sensations she swayed uneasily on her feet. 'Can I open them?'

'No. Trust me, *cara mia,*' he said, voice smouldering as he gently took her hands and laid them flat against…a wall.

Then his fingers were at her nape and he slowly untied the sash of her bikini top. No wires, it wrapped around her breasts sash-like and tied at her nape. A tie he was languidly unravelling with practised hands. *Oh, God.*

'Breathe,' he said with calm severity and she inhaled long and low—the fresh scent of raw earth, Mother Nature at its finest weaving through her head, smoky like an image of opium mist. 'Do not be afraid of your body. Let it speak to you.'

Bones now lax, her other senses heightened, she felt the material give way, the heavy weight of her breasts pull on her shoulders. Then the soft material slithered around her face, vanquishing any remaining light behind her eyelids.

Blindfolded.

No fear. Just anticipation thrumming through her veins. Life beating in her heart.

'What can you feel?' he said in that husky murmur that made her heart thump faster, harder. 'Because you like to touch, don't you, *tesoro*.'

'Heat everywhere,' she said, her voice a quiver, rasping past her dry lips. 'As if…I'm stood in an inferno blasted from every angle. So hot. So sticky.'

'More—tell me more,' he said, breath ragged as he splayed her legs with his large hands.

'Sand tickling the soles of my feet. Cool and wet. Slipping, *sliding* between my toes. Rock biting into my palms. Coarse. Craggy. And now…' She gasped, shook with the force of his devilish touch. 'Your big warm hands curving around my waist, spanning, gripping…flaring wide over my stomach…sneaking under my waistband.'

Legs turning to water, she leaned forward, bracing her full weight on the wall. 'You're taking them off,' she whispered on a tremulous breath.

A thrilling ripple of wicked titillation sizzled over every inch of her skin, set fire to her veins. Sweat trickled down her spine. So hot. So very hot.

'I am. Slowly, teasingly, sliding the damp clinging fabric down your beautiful long legs. I dream of these legs, *tesoro*. Around my waist. My neck. And, *Cristo*, if they do not kill me, your lush firm behind just might.'

His long dextrous fingers shimmied down her legs, pushing her bikini to the floor and then he kissed, *oh*, he kissed and moulded his hands to her calves, lapped the backs of her knees with his velvet tongue.

A primal groan, long and deep, rumbled from the depths of his chest as he lapped and kissed the curve of her bottom, gently nibbled up her spine, pressing his lush wet mouth over every inch of her skin. Until she was boneless. Pliant. Completely at his mercy.

'That's it, *cara*, give yourself to me.'

Eva crushed her lips. Fearing it was too late. Far too late. She'd given herself to him long ago. Dante

Vitale had owned her from first glance. *No, no, Eva. Don't even think it.*

Panic flared behind her left breast…but when his hand slid back around her waist, glissaded up her torso and gently cupped the heavy weight, panic was replaced by the fervour for pressure and she pushed into his hand. *Oh, boy.*

A guttural groan tore from his throat. '*Maledizione*, Eva.' His foot pushed the inside of her calf—first one, then the other—forcing her legs wider. 'More.' And she did exactly that, shuffling across the sand, widening her stance, bending more at the waist, the jagged rock now lancing her palms.

'You have the most beautiful back I have ever seen,' he said, his Italian accent now deliciously raw as if the polished exterior was being buffed away. 'Every dip, every curve, provocative perfection.' He scraped his blunt fingernails across her shoulders, down her vertebrae and Eva threw her head back, arching sinuously.

Perfection? Did he really mean that? She wanted to ask but it sounded so needy. And she hated need. Knowing the only person she could rely on was herself.

'What do you feel?' he growled.

'You. Everywhere.' And he was. Flush tight at

her back, she could feel his thick erection, hard and demanding behind his swim shorts.

Without conscious thought, she lifted one hand from the cold craggy rock, reached behind her and smoothed down his sweat-drenched honed stomach to touch him. Hot. So hot. Hard. So very hard. He must be in agony. So she curled her fingers around his thick length, determined to entice, but he jerked from her touch.

'No,' he said, with his raw, unrelenting force of will. 'This is about your pleasure, not mine, *cara mia.*'

Before she could think of a retort to tempt him, he rolled her nipple between the pads of his fingers—gentle, hesitant—luring a moan from her parched throat.

With every touch, he waited for her reaction, testing, teasing. And her heart, *God*, her heart ached. Why was he doing this for her? Why did he care?

His thumb dusted over her small scar and Eva stiffened, waiting for the threads of tension to pull in her stomach. A tug that never came.

'So brave, *tesoro,*' he murmured. 'Do not let this remind you of what has passed or what may come. Let it remind you how strong you are. That you have fight in every breath you take. How you must live in the moment, make every second count.'

Tears stung the backs of her eyes like tiny daggers. 'Dante…' *I'm scared.*

'No fear, Eva. No more fear. Promise me this. Whatever happens,' he said huskily, smoothing his big hand down her midriff and laying his palm on her tummy in that way that tore a yearning through her heart, 'no more fear.'

Another command. Another touch. To enrapture. Inflame. Banishing all thought. All fear. Until she could no longer resist the heady pressure making her insides twitch, the blood thrum through her body. More intense than ever before. Dante flicked his thumb over her nipple, sending another bright hot spark firing to her core. And, 'Oh, God, Dante I…'

'What, *cara mia*?'

'When you do that…'

He did it again, bit into her shoulder, soothed the bite with the velvet flat of his tongue, cupped both her breasts in his hands and oh-so-lightly squeezed the soft flesh.

Wham—her body shook and sparked with the first flicker of an orgasm—an orgasm the likes of which she'd never known. And the air whooshed from her lungs as she tried to fight it off.

'*Cristo*, Eva,' he said, before murmuring hushed Italian in her ear, making her stomach scrunch, her orgasm coil tighter. God, she wished she knew what he was saying. It was the same words every time he made love to her, she was sure. Words that spoke to her heart. 'Let go.'

Another demand, blurring her vision, her mind. Until her body took over, stomach concaving with the force of the building pressure and Eva pushed her bottom towards him, seeking, a wanton cry gushing from her throat. 'Dante, *please.*'

Trembling, she hovered at the edge of heaven—or was it hell?—and heard him swear long and low. Still like cast bronze. Then shudder as if he fought some kind of evil, an internal battle, grappling with the reins of his control.

'Eva, do not beg me, *cara*,' he said, voice harder than the rock beneath her fingers. 'No protection.'

Silence. Just the soft trickle of water in the distance, the heavy beat of her heart echoing in her ears.

Silence. As if they both waited for the other to speak. *So take me, take another risk. I want you so much.*

Silence. *Speak to me, please. Tell me what you're thinking...*

A sigh, laced with resignation, dusted over her

nape. Soft skin he graced with a kiss, so ardent it was almost devout as he gently flicked his thumb over her tight nipple and slid his other hand down her stomach, murmuring, 'Let go, *cara*.' He thrust two fingers inside of her, growling in her ear, 'Let. Go.'

Wham—she splintered into a million pieces, every bone cracking with the force of the orgasm tearing through her like a tornado.

'*Dante*,' she cried. Because it went on and on, whipping the air from her lungs, swirling every thought in her mind and lifting her so high she literally feared the cataclysmic drop. And still he was relentless. Thrusting his fingers in and out as she clenched and spasmed around his hand, her body convulsing, racked with pleasure.

Falling, falling, her legs buckled and Dante's hand slipped from her breast to wrap around her waist holding her upright with iron strength.

'I won't let you fall. I swear it,' he said with such fierceness she glimpsed a hidden meaning. If she could just think past the carnal oblivion...

'Again, *tesoro*.'

'I...I can't.'

'*Sì*, you can,' he said with dark intensity as he pushed inside her, hand now flexing, curling, cupping—simultaneously teasing her buttons inside and out while his heat seared her back. 'So beautiful, Eva, so very beautiful.' And his mouth licked and bit her shoulder and his thick erection nuzzled the crease of her bottom and—

Wham—another orgasm ripped through her core, all molten heat and liquid fire, tearing her apart, burning, scorching her lungs until she felt like a living, breathing flame.

Stripped to her soul, at that moment she knew the truth. She'd been lying to herself all along.

Dante Vitale owned her. Heart, body and soul. Always had. Always would.

So when her head began to spin with black ribbons and the ground lifted to meet her, she said the only thing she could. The only thing to thwart the words leeching from her heart, words embedded since she was eighteen years old. *I love you…*

'I surrender.'

CHAPTER THIRTEEN

SHIVERING VIOLENTLY, EVA roused from delirious possession to find herself straddling Dante's lap as he sat on the floor of the cave, his long legs stretched out beneath her.

Body lax, mind weak, she buried her face in his neck and surrendered to his ministrations as he wrapped her bikini sash around her breasts and tied a knot at her nape with a soothing amorous touch.

Air. She needed air. So hot. So dizzy. But, as she filled her lungs, all she could smell, all she could taste was his signature masculine scent: bergamot with lashings of the blackest amber. Dark. So very dark.

Dante raised his knees off the ground behind her and her body slipped forward until they were slick—skin against skin—and instinctively she clung to him like a life raft as he wrapped his arms around her, rocking with a gentle persuasion. As if she was his most prized possession. Such a foolish thought, her defences kicked in to frisk her skin with apprehension and shoot sanity into her mind.

Surrendering her heart to him was one thing, didn't mean she was insane enough to imagine he returned the strength of her feelings. So she didn't want to cling to him. Or need him.

I won't let you fall. I swear it…

Space. She needed space. To think. To breathe. The lines were blurring hazier by the second.

Lifting her face from the crook of his neck, she pushed at his chest, swivelling her shoulders to twist free of the steel cage of his arms. And if a tiny part of her wanted him to hold on—to never let her go—that tiny part was crushed when he immediately released her.

'Can you stand, *tesoro*?' he asked, his voice raspy, dry.

Oh, boy. Pricked with embarrassment at the way she'd lost it, she tore her face from his view and coerced her legs to wake with a gentle flex. 'I think so.'

Curving those big hands around her waist, he lifted her to her feet, holding her in place as she tested her weight. Then, *oh, boy*, she made the mistake of looking down and his face was right *there* and…where the hell were her bikini bottoms? 'I'm fine,' she croaked. 'Really.'

Eva took a step back and leaned against the cool wet rock as Dante pushed himself up in one graceful athletic movement and swept his hands down the backs of his thighs, sand flicking in every direction.

Only then did she notice. 'Black sand.' She gave a little huff. Of course it was. What else would Dante Vitale's caves be lined with but volcanic sand?

'Wait here,' he said, veering around a corner, disappearing from view.

Within seconds her eyes were darting around the floor for a gold scrap and, *Thank you, God*, she whipped the sodden bottoms up her legs, cringing at the gritty chafe, just in time to see Dante reappear—sports duffel in hand—both owner and bag drenched.

Despite the cold seeping into her feet, she felt her lips twitch. 'Bottom of the lake, huh?'

He gave her one of those half bad-boy smiles that threatened the already precarious state of her knees as he unscrewed the cap of a water bottle and passed it to her.

Eva relished the cool liquid pouring down her tight throat.

'I believe I promised you heaven on earth,' he

said, pointing to a gap in the rock before he placed the clear rim of his bottle on his lower lip…

The sight of his smooth throat convulsing acted like another blast of heat and Eva yanked the elastic hairband from her wrist, lifted the hair stuck to her nape and piled it on top of her head in a messy knot. With a quick fix of the band, she turned back to see him staring at her. Oddly.

'What?'

Brushing the back of his hand over his wet mouth, he shook his head. 'Your hair like that… reminds me of when I first saw you.'

Eva gave him a kick of her brow. Typical man. His memory was way off.

'My hair was down that day. At the tennis courts at home. You were playing with Finn and…' Eva and her friends had been glued. Mesmerised by all that yummy darkness and athletic grace. And now she'd just told him that the memory was imprinted on her brain!

Dante crossed his arms over his wide chest, shoulders bunching, pecs bulging. 'That wasn't the first time I saw you.'

Eva blinked. He had his own memory imprint? 'It wasn't?'

'No,' he said simply, then nodded in the general

direction of the sliver. 'Go ahead, *tesoro*. Ladies first.'

Gaze flicking from the gap back to him, she questioned the intelligence of asking him more. Would have if he hadn't trailed his fingers down to the small of her back, her flesh quivering under the deft stroke, and gave her a little push.

Angled sideways, she breathed in and slithered through the gap, almost collapsing with relief when she made it to a wider opening, the blinding light making her recoil with a deep squint.

Anticipation was a *thump thump* of her heart, feet tentative to eke out the suspense as she gingerly made her way to the jagged archway. Sight slowly adjusting, the first sound that whispered through her mind was one of water trickling, pooling. The second was the chirp and song of a small bird, waning with the flutter of tiny wings. And the third was the echo of leaves—not thin and crisp like an autumn rustle but saturated with dewy flesh from the heights of summer.

Coarse grainy sand gave way to the tickle of scented grass and she shielded the sun's rays with one hand…and gasped, warm air snatching at her throat. '*Oh*, Dante.'

As if God had used a giant spoon and scooped

a hole from the rock, they were stood at the base, surrounded by breathtaking beauty.

Waterfalls cascading, gushing into an azure lake. Trees in lush bloom, weeping exotic fruits and trailing pink and cerise flowers in elongated spirals to kiss the lush bed beneath. A butterfly fluttered past her face with wings of orange and lilac and settled on the rich green meadow smothered in tiny white flowers.

'It…it's like *Fantasia*. I didn't think places like this even existed.' The divine beauty was another physical blow and, without knowing how or why, tears stung the backs of her eyes. She had to turn her face from his view and blink rapidly to dissolve the mist.

'Hey,' he said, curving his hand around her jaw and tempting her back to meet thick dark lashes surrounding eyes that glittered. 'Do not hide your emotions from me. If it makes you feel better, I was also overwhelmed when I discovered it for myself.'

'Have you brought…?' She stopped herself in the nick of time, suddenly afraid he'd seduced a multitude of women here.

'Only you.' He brushed down her nose with the back of his index finger, then strode over to a large tree, heavy with fruit and flora. Reaching up, he plucked a large white flower from a cluster of dark purple oval fruit.

'Is that passion fruit?' she asked whilst *Only you* rang in her ears.

'A loose translation would be tryst-fruit. Very similar in taste and texture, but immensely potent,' he said, walking back towards her, his shorts clinging to his perfectly buff body as he twirled the flower stem between his thumb and index finger.

'Like a…an aphrodisiac?' No way was she eating that stuff. Dante was potent enough and she could barely think straight as it was.

'*Sì.*'

As he drew near, the sun glinted and shimmered off the long silky tropical petals. 'It looks like an orchid.'

'I know you do not like flowers,' he said.

'Who said I didn't like—?' She winced inwardly, remembering the tongue-lashing she gave him last week. 'Oh, well, I was angry with you. Asking your secretary to fill my boutique is totally different to…to…' Trailing off, she stared into his eyes as he slid the fine stalk down her cleavage, snug behind her sash, the tiny scratch making her breath hitch.

'To what, *cara mia*?' he murmured, his fingertips grazing across the low scooped edge of her bikini, teasing. A little higher to her bare breast. Tempting.

Her eyelashes grew heavy as he cupped her with a gentle touch. Then his head dipped to the heavy aching flesh as he peeled back the gold fabric and...*oh*, he kissed her small scar. Once. Twice. Softly. Devout.

Paradise vanished behind her eyelids and her hand trembled with the need to reach up, push him into her, hold him close. And her heart...her heart gushed, overflowed.

'Different to...you choosing,' she whispered on a fluttering breath, chest heaving, 'a flower.' As a flock of butterflies began to sweep and swerve into her stomach. *Careful, Eva, you've been here before. Nothing is what it seems.*

Yet, when he lifted his head and caught her eyes, he was going to tell her something. She could virtually see his internal struggle. *Tell me, tell me. Give me something more than vague signs. Give me words. Actual words. That I can hear. That I can believe. Give me truth. Please.*

Backing up a pace, he flexed his shoulders, his posture making it clear she was pleading for the impossible, and her stomach plunged to the grass.

'This *Fantasia*, as you call it,' he said, the educated-at-Cambridge formality back in line as he set stride towards the lake, 'is one of the reasons I bought the island. Untouched, its innocence, purity called to me on some level.' His footsteps slowed and he tilted his head until she was awarded with his uber-masculine profile. 'I, the darkest, coldest of men, some say the most ruthless on earth, own such a place.' Swivelling with the predatory grace of a sleek black panther, he shot her with a killer look. 'Amusing, don't you think?'

Eva blinked. Wondering if this was some kind of trick question. Yet, from the fierce expression on his face, her opinion mattered to him.

'No, I think it's wonderful.' It spoke of his beating heart. Although, in all fairness, she would never have expected Dante to own a place so hopeful, romantic. The flip side to his cynicism, his darkness. It was bewildering. Enchanting. 'Whoever said you are cold has never met you, Dante.' Yes, he was ruthless and controlling, but cold? No. He wasn't cold. He was white-hot heat.

'I guarantee this woman knew me very well, *cara*.'

Eva crushed her lips together. 'Oh. Your ex-wife.'

His brow nipped in a split second of confusion as if she had it wrong, but then he shrugged nonchalantly.

Curling her fingers, she dug her nails into her

palm. She didn't like thinking about his marriage. It made her a little jealous. Okay, insanely jealous.

Which was just ridiculous considering she had a good idea of what Natalia's life would have been like. An arid wasteland of craving for this man's love and affection.

What had he said? *Cold.*

'Why did you marry her?'

'My father desired the match. A joining of two old Italian families. One I had resisted for a long time.' The way he looked at her right then— haunted, possessive—sent a shiver scuttling over the back of her thighs. 'In hindsight, it was doomed from the start.'

'It sounds…cold.'

'Arctic, *cara*,' he said, hard, irascible. *Cold.* Then *slam*, the shutters fell down over his face. Conversation over.

Eva tried for a swallow and tugged the orchid from her cleavage, but as she looked into the pink folds shrouding the heart she realised she wasn't willing to part with it. Just yet.

Dante and her were anything but cold, right? Right.

Threading the flower through the knot in her hair, she took a tentative step towards him as he crouched down at the water's edge and dipped his hand into the depths as if testing the temperature.

'The people from the mainland call it Dream Falls,' he said, voice thick and edged with cynicism. 'They say if you make a wish in the waters, your dream will come true.'

'Do you believe that?'

'It does not matter what I believe. But in my experience dreams are born from hard work and determination.'

Eva's feet froze a few paces away as she closed her eyes and sighed. 'Vitale. Taking Vitale to stratospheric heights. That's why you work night and day.' It was all about Vitale. Every move he made. It was like an addiction. An obsession. Ruling his every waking thought.

'*Sì.*'

'Why? Money? Power? Don't you have enough of both?'

'I care nothing for wealth.' He fingered his damp hair until it spiked and flicked in its usual effortless sexy mess and stared across the rippling waters. 'It is a question of self-worth. Pride. You take great pride in being successful at your work, do you not?'

'Yes, of course. But…you're one of the most successful men in the world and still you keep going.

What are you trying to prove to yourself?' While Eva loved her job, she knew half of what drove her was the need to make her mother proud. 'Or does it have more to do with your father?'

The muscles in his shoulders visibly tensed, his jaw locking with an audible click. And she could feel the pain emanating from him in a pulsating wave. 'There is no pleasing such a man, *cara*. I do it for myself.'

He was either lying to himself or her. Against his better judgement, he'd even married Natalia to please him.

No thought, no hesitation, she walked to the edge and sat upon the grassy lip, allowing her legs to plunge into the clear liquid.

Dante swung down to sit beside her, his tight muscular thigh dusted with dark hair mere inches away from her soft milky skin. She waited a beat, choosing her words carefully, knowing she trod in dark, dangerous depths. 'I guess you went to live with him when your mother died.'

A small jerk of his head was her only reply and she played with the grass, tearing a few blades from the root. *Easy, Eva.*

Sprinkling the grass into the water, she watched it float, drift on the slight breeze. Thinking of a perfectly natural question. 'When will I get to meet him? After all, one day he might be a grandfather.'

Dante's head shot up, eyes, fierce and deadly, careening into hers, his skin taut where he leashed the beast within. 'Hear this, Eva. I do not want my child *anywhere* near him. Nor you. *Capisci*?'

And with that brutal howling declaration came not only a plunge of unease but also the memory of his ferocious protective streak when they spoke of their child.

I will be there for our child... I am strong and powerful enough to shield him from every storm.

Licking her dry lips, she swallowed hard. 'Was he...brutal?'

'Only with his tongue, *cara*,' he said, his voice hard enough to smash glass. 'Although, in truth, at times, I would've preferred a fist.'

Crushing her lips, she closed her eyes momentarily. No matter how hard she tried, she couldn't stop her imagination firing a tirade of nasty insults and a chill pervaded her bones.

'Do you still see him on Vitale business?'

'*Sì*. But he no longer controls my world. I control his. The power is mine. Vitale was drowning when I took over and now it is also *mine*. And always will be.'

Of course he wanted control. After a life dictated by others, who wouldn't?

The silence stretched, her patience with it, until she reached up, smoothed his jaw, coaxing with a gentle hand. When their eyes met, her lips parted on an indrawn breath.

Such frustration. Such pain. God, what kind of childhood must he have had?

Fifteen years old and he'd buried his volatile mother, only to be faced with a monster specialising in mental anguish. Thrust into a heartless world—a world he'd been denied. To live with total strangers. A continual fight for his position, for the worth and self-respect his father had denied him. Was it any wonder he was so closed off from his emotions? She fancied they were buried so deep he would explode with one rattle of the key. Often times she could feel his body vibrating with power, as if they all churned inside him, threatening to burst free.

It didn't take a genius to figure out how he controlled them all. Anger. It was his first defence.

Gently, she brushed a damp lock of hair from his sun-kissed brow. 'Ah, Dante. Finally, I see you,' she said, using the exact same words he'd said to her only yesterday.

For she knew the desperation, the need to prove

her worth, to prove to the world she was more than just a daughter of famous parents. More than Diva, the party girl who had drifted astray. Hadn't she spent the last week trying to prove herself to him?

Soul aching, she said in a wild whisper, 'Listen to me. I don't know one other man who could reach the heights of your success. I hope you are very proud.' Rubbing her thumb over his soft fleshy bottom lip, her mind drifted. 'What did you say to me this morning? About the good memories of my mum and dad. You said: *keep the good memories in your heart*. So I say take all your achievements, your successes and hold them in your heart. And be proud of yourself.'

Leaning forward, she kissed the corner of his mouth. 'Don't allow him to rule your life any longer. Rise above him, Dante, far, far above him where you belong. Promise me.'

For long moments he stared into her eyes. One long loaded look, the connection so startlingly intense, the world seemed to compress around them. As if they were the only two living souls on the planet. A look that said a million things and, like the mysteries of the universe, she understood none of them.

A shadow crept over her shoulder, smothering the light. As if the sun had been usurped by thick ominous clouds and a new emotion penetrated the haze.

Fear. She could feel fear in the air. Coating her skin, cool and clammy, until she struggled to breathe. It clutched at her heart and it was all from her—she knew it *must* be. Yet there was something in his eyes, those fathomless dark eyes— a look she'd seen once before—but she couldn't place it, no matter how hard she tried. So elusive. So out of reach.

And that only served to heighten her frustration. Her fear. Because, for the second time in her life, she was about to put her heart on the line for him. Such folly, she knew. But it was this place. Bewitching. Beguiling her with hope when she knew it was bad for her soul. It was his words: *how strong you are...no more fear.* Giving her strength. When she felt weak as a newborn foal.

A tremor started in her toes, swept up her legs and, before it reached her hand, she took it from his face. Twisted her fingers in the well of her lap. 'Don't you ever want more? More than Vitale? More than success?'

From nowhere the breeze turned volatile. Wind slammed into her back to send strands of hair blowing around her face and her eyes closed in defence. Reaching up, she swept her brow and,

when she opened her eyes once more, Dante's unyielding jaw was locked tight, the muscle protest-
ing fiercely. 'What else is there to live for, Eva?'

Do it, Eva. Say it. Say it. Be brave. Be strong.

Raising her legs from the water, she hugged her
wet knees to her chest and tried for a nonchalant
shrug. 'I don't know. Love?'

Out went the light in his eyes, even his bronzed
skin visibly paled. 'Love is not possible for a man
like me.'

Eva nodded slowly, her bones colder than they'd
ever been before. *You're such a fool, Eva.*

She'd been lying to herself, thinking she could
marry him and stop herself from wanting more,
from craving his love. When, in truth, that was
all she wanted. All she'd ever wanted. His heart.

And that made her feel selfish and shameful because gaining his love would only bring him pain
if she fell sick.

Oh, God, she was a horrible, horrible person because she wanted the whispering promises of this
idyllic Utopia. The fairy tale. What her mum and
dad shared all those years ago. The love *this* man
made her remember. She wanted it all.

Sadness crept into her chest until each breath
ached and she bowed her head, resting her brow
on her knees, the future suddenly a scary place.

Because, yes, she desperately wanted to be pregnant, to have *his* baby, but that would lead her to a marriage bed that would surely turn as cold as his first, as she craved for his love and affection. Leaving her vulnerable. Heart, shattered fragments of pain.

The wind picked up pace, whipping around her, smacking off her wet legs, nipping her skin. Lifting her head, she focused on the surface of the water, the ripples now deep from the hard lick of the breeze.

Crushing her lips, she rocked back and forth, the hard ground biting into her flesh. 'Why did you bring me here, Dante?' *Why did you make me fall again?*

'I knew you would appreciate such vivid beauty,' he said easily, oblivious to the storm raging inside her. 'I will gift it to you if you wish.'

Eva snapped round to face him, ignorant of the pain shooting up her neck. 'Gift it?' Like when he bought jewellery for his bed-partners as a fond farewell?

'*Sì*. As a wedding gift.'

'You seem awfully sure I'm pregnant, Dante.'

He shrugged those arrogant shoulders. 'I am.'

'You really want this baby, don't you?'

'*Sì*. Very much. I have wished for an heir for a long time. It will be a dream come true for me.'

Every muscle in her body froze—*an heir*?

Mind spinning like a bobbin wheel, she began to reel in threads. 'That's why you married Natalia, isn't it? Not only to please your father but for an heir.'

'Of course. Why else?'

Oh, boy. Here she'd been dreaming of churches and christening gowns and Dante had pounced for an heir. From the start it had been about Vitale and he'd lured her in like the Pied Piper whistling his flute. First for the sake of Hamptons and now a possible heir to the Vitale empire.

My God, she could see it now. She'd bet the first thing that popped into his mind after the anger had abated from not using protection was: *Heir. Vitale. Vitale.*

And he intended to placate her with what? Sex and an island?

'I imagine it's worth quite a bit,' she said, not entirely sure what the hell she was playing at. Only knowing she wanted him to hurt like she did.

'Several million,' he said. 'It is easy enough to arrange. I can have the marriage contracts adjusted by sunset if you so desire.'

Everything stopped.

Her breasts began to rise and fall in heavy waves, while he just sat there. Pensive. Gazing across the lake. Clearly thinking of his precious Vitale. And her throat—*God*, her throat was stinging with the prick of a thousand pins.

For a split second she considered the idea she was overreacting. Being irrational. Ditched that idea right in his damn lake!

'You had papers drawn up?' she said, her voice escalating with every word. 'Like…a business contract? *Already*?'

With eerily slow movements, he turned to face her, one dark insolent brow raised over his intense glare. '*Sì*, this morning. Is there a problem?'

Eva shuffled along the grassy lip, creating distance.

She'd told him all her secrets, all her fears and he'd made love to her, shattered her every defence until she'd opened her heart. And all she'd wanted was for him to hold her and instead he'd left her in bed. Alone. To draw up a…a *marriage contract*? 'How can anyone be so cold? Heartless.'

His beautiful, despicable head jerked as if she'd slapped him. Right now, she couldn't care less.

'Why a contract, Dante?' she said as an insidious notion slithered into her mind. 'Don't you trust me?'

'It is not a question of trust.'

'Oh, yes, it is.' Clearly, he didn't trust her. After all that had happened between them. He still didn't trust her. And, *oh, God*, that hurt. 'What exactly does this contract protect your heir against?' She thought back to his mother, his childhood—his awful volatile childhood—and her heart wept for him but what did she have to do to prove herself?

Pique, which must have been as plain as the nose on her face because his brow scrunched, eyes raking over her. 'Eva, you are looking at this the wrong way. It will protect us all. You will be financially secure—'

'But I don't want your money, Dante!' she said, hating the quiver in her voice as she scrambled to her feet, stumbling backward, water dripping down her calves. 'And I will not marry a man who does not trust me. It's all so cold. I am not one of your stores to buy or tie up in a business contract. You can't control my life.'

Worst thing was, she couldn't even hate him for trying.

The gorgeous man put more faith in business contracts, what he could actually control, than the power of emotion or even human nature. So many people had let him down in his life he trusted no one. He'd become impenetrable.

Whoosh, he was up on his feet, towering over her, all six-foot-three of male dominance and seething fury.

'Hear this, Eva,' he growled, feral waves pouring off his buff frame and his eyes… There was something terrifying about the splintering power of his gaze. 'If you are pregnant we *will* marry. You may have no choice.'

'Oh, believe me, I do have a choice. That's one thing you can't control. Baby or no baby, I will never marry you.' The words lanced her throat, for how many times had she dreamed of marrying this man? But not like this.

Clouds, thick with anger, rolled across the sky and Eva felt the first drops of rain pelt her flesh.

'We discussed the need for marriage, Eva,' he bit out.

'Well, suddenly I don't care about the reputation I've fought so long and hard for. People will just have to take me as I am. I don't care about what the papers say about me. I know the truth. What's more important is that I can live with myself. So I will stand tall and tell Finn that the fault is mine alone.'

Thunder rumbled up his heaving chest before he struck her down with a bolt of lightning. 'You *know* how important it is to me that my child has my name. You gave me your word, Eva. And you question why I do not trust?'

Pat, pat went the rain, the heavy beat punishing, trickling a path down her shoulders, her chest, dousing the flaming sparks of her ire.

'I know, I'm sorry. But…don't you see? It isn't about names. It isn't about marrying me to prevent history repeating itself. You have to trust me. I'm *not* your mother. And you're *not* your father. He was a dishonourable man. A terrible dad. But you…you have honour. Integrity. Never have I doubted for a second that you wouldn't stand by me. You would be a great Dad. You're *nothing* like him.'

Shaking his head fiercely, he threw his muscular arms wide. 'Then why break your word? Why refuse to marry?'

She covered her heart with the flat of her hand. 'Because I want love. I want to get married in a beautiful little church and speak vows from my heart and know that the man standing beside me loves me for who I am. *Not* what I can give him. I want the fairy tale and I'll never have that with you.'

Dante's arms dropped to his sides, hands clenched, a look bordering on torment tightening his features. 'One night. You got your one night, Eva,' he said thickly. 'Five years late, but you got it.'

Eva stroked up her chest, fingers curling around her throat. If she wasn't mistaken, she would say he was hurt. No. Surely not. How could she possibly have the power to hurt him?

'I'm so sorry.'

Hands trembling, she closed her fingertips round her engagement ring and slipped off the heavy band. Unable to look at the beauty, the promise. Unable to even think about the words he'd whispered to her that day. Knowing she would crack in two.

Nothing is too much for the woman of my heart, tesoro.

Feet squelching on the sodden grass, she took two steps forward…took his hand, placed her ring in his palm and stumbled back. 'As soon as I know, I'll tell you. I believe I have all three of your business numbers after all.'

All that riveting beauty schooled into impassivity before her very eyes.

'Very well,' he said, throwing her ring into the air and catching it in the same hand, his lips twisting with that cynicism it had taken her a week to erase.

She just thanked God for Mother Nature's wrath

because the rain now fell in heavy lashing sheets, pouring down her face. Blending, hiding the warm tears streaming down her face.

Flick, up the yellow diamond spun once more, glinting in the air as he turned to walk away…and her heart cracked in two as she heard the soft *plop* of hope, of the fairy tale, falling, falling, falling into the dark depths of the lake.

CHAPTER FOURTEEN

Two weeks later...

DANTE WRESTLED WITH the thick knot of his cerise tie, shoved his icy finger down the tight space between neck and collar and tore the top button of his white shirt free. Staring at the solid oak, he asked himself again—why? Why couldn't he knock on her door?

Cristo, he was cold. Cold through to the pit of his stomach. Colder than the dense blanket of new-fallen snow outside her boutique, colder than the now clear liquid pooling on the floor around his Italian leather–soled feet.

And, *Dannazione*, he ached. Ached only for her.

For the first time in his life he was terrified. And, as the night drew to a close, he beat and berated himself for wandering around the city— his benighted soul oblivious to the Christmas Eve cheer—preparing mental speeches, which for the life of him he couldn't recall.

Rolling his shoulders, he inhaled slow and deep. Raised his hand and rapped on the door, once, twice, bracing his taut body for the cataclysmic impact of simply taking one look.

The sound of metal sliding across metal filtered from inside and scored his sensitized skin like talons down a chalkboard. And when the solid oak swung wide…his heart stopped. Dead.

There she was. Tousled. With that adorable sleepy look about her. The one that made him remember and covet all at once.

Eva St George.

Twenty-seven years old and more beautiful than ever. All that gorgeous caramel hair a tumble of lavish waves framing her exquisite face. A warm dove-grey jersey dress clung to her lush curves, delineating the fine bones of her décolletage, the long sleeves framing her delicate wrists and the straight-cut hem kissing her knees. But, *Cristo*, it was the bare feet that really snagged him. Perfect little toes painted pearly-white, as if she walked on heavenly clouds. And there it was again. That hint of innocence he now *knew* to be truth.

Dante closed his eyes. Inhaled a lungful of air that was a physical pain in his tight chest…

'Hello, Dante.'

…And his pulse skyrocketed into the one hundred and sixties when her soft husky voice crashed into his psyche with the ferocity of a sledgehammer.

Only then did he focus on her flawless face. Pale, she was so pale. Grey smudges of dark days and darker nights weighty beneath her eyes.

A giant fist gripped his guts, punched his heart. '*Cristo*, Eva. Are you sick?'

Huge green eyes darted over his face, her brow nipping tight. 'I was just about to ask you the same thing.'

'I do not care about me, *cara*, are you unwell?' He stepped over the threshold, hand up to feel her brow…a crucifying claw tearing at his insides, when she shrank away from his touch.

Dante stepped back. But not before he caught her pure soft scent, arousing him, clouding his brain.

'I'm not sick, Dante,' she said on a trembling rush, 'just tired. I haven't stopped since—'

'*Sì*, of course. Congratulations, *cara*. An Arunthian Princess is quite a coup d'etat.'

She tried for a small smile. 'We met at a charity dinner. I pushed for a chance to draw up some designs. She adored them. Most of my consultations came off too.'

'I am so proud of you, *tesoro*.'

'Thank you,' she whispered, placing her hand on the soft curve of her stomach, as if she ached. That tiny movement a bolt of lightning cracking through the brume in his mind.

It was tactless and he knew she would suspect it was the only reason he was here, but, 'Do you know if you are…?'

Crushing her lips, she gave a small shake of her head and a tumult of conflicting emotions swirled inside of him. A crushing regret that she would never carry his child. Pain that he would never see her after this night. And a sharp sense of relief that he could tell her the truth without her questioning his sincerity.

'Twenty minutes, Eva. That is all I ask.'

A soft blush heated her cheeks and it took him less than a second to know its genesis. The cave. Twenty minutes for her surrender. He knew better than to hope for it again. Or even to try. This time there would be no tempting or deal-making. Only truth.

'I would like to explain,' he said hoarsely. 'To tell you something. Then I will leave and I swear I will never bother you again.'

Sweat, cold and clammy, smothered his back as he waited for her answer, his eyes narrowing on the flutter of her hand as she massaged her temple, as if he were a headache she wished to rub away.

'Okay,' she said, standing back to allow him in. 'Twenty minutes.'

Before relief stole the purpose from his stride, Dante closed the door behind him with a soft click and followed her through to the lounge, ordering his eyes to stay above her sculpted waist before visions of lacy white panties cupping her gorgeous behind enraptured his mind, stole his sanity.

Cosy. Homely. The lounge was delicately lit by a floor lamp casting shadowy patterns over her eclectic tastes. A tall scented Christmas fir stood before the window, bare. Open boxes of colourful glittering baubles, blown-glass love-hearts and golden cherubs, littered the floor, full. The Edwardian hearth blazed a roaring fire, the crackle and spit of wood enhancing the aroma of fresh pine, warming his bones.

'I have disturbed your decorating. I am sorry it is late to call, Eva, but I have been to see Yakatani—'

'Of course you have,' she said ruefully, curling up on the sofa in her usual snuggled fashion, the sight making his chest clench and this time he knew the reason why. He wanted her to snuggle into *him*. Find comfort in *him*.

Her small sigh quivered in the air. 'I didn't mean

that to sound off. I'm happy for you, Dante, really I am.'

'I did not sign for Hamptons, Eva.'

Long hazel lashes blinked up at him, her full lips parted, working around words. 'Why not?'

This was it. The culmination of two weeks, tearing himself apart wondering how the hell he'd managed to make such a mess of everything.

Dante eyed the sofa cushion beside her, decided it was pushing his don't-touch limits to the extreme. The chair was too far away because she needed to see his eyes. So…

He sat on the coffee table in front of her, a clean two feet between them, braced his elbows on his knees, clasped his hands to stop from reaching, touching, hauling her to him and locked on to her huge wary eyes.

'Because you were right,' he said, his throat so thick he could hear the low rasp of his voice. 'My father denied my very existence until my mother died and he was forced to take me in. To say his legitimate family were coloured with hate is an understatement, *cara*. Remember when we spoke of you and your father burying pain?'

Brow nipped tight, eyes brimming with empathy, she gave him a jerky nod.

'I buried mine in Vitale. For the last fifteen years

I worked night and day to prove that I was worthy of being one of them. That I was not tainted by my mother's bad blood. Hamptons was the jewel in my crown.' He stopped. Took a huge gulping breath. 'But, when it came down to it, I would rather make *you* proud of me. I would rather prove my worth to *you*. For you, my beautiful, loyal, selfless Eva, are more worthy of the effort and sentiment than my father will ever be. I wanted to prove to you that you would always come before Vitale. And I will not have you feeling discomfort from telling untruths for my sake.'

Her chest hitched as if she'd been holding her breath, her words no more than a whisper. 'You... you told him?'

'The truth about us, *Sì.*'

Sucking her full lips in as if to stifle a sob, she shook her head. 'I can't believe you did that for me.'

Feet flat to the floor, he had to stiffen his muscles to stop himself reaching, taking her, never letting go. But he needed to say this. Because the pain of holding it in was killing him and he'd been lying to himself, and her, all along.

No more fear.

'I would do anything for you, Eva.'

Her heavy breasts rose and fell, but she never left

his gaze. Eyes that were the key to his soul… One turn in the lock and all the tension drained from his body, the words, the truth, rushing out of him.

'I would give everything I own for one more day with you. I would sell my soul to keep you well. If you got sick I would trade my life for yours.'

One glistening tear trickled down her smooth cheek but nothing was stopping him now—

'What I cannot do is make you love me. And that, my beautiful angel, was the true reason I had those contracts drawn. I tried to tell myself it was because I did not trust you. But in truth I was afraid and I was trying to keep you by my side. Tied to me without the bonds of love. Hoping the inevitable would not happen.'

She dashed away her tears with the back of her hand. 'What are you…? What inevitable?'

He felt a weary smile tilt his mouth. 'Anyone who looked at one of your dresses, Eva, would know you wanted the fairy tale. You were fighting it. Because of your father. The risk to your health. Deep down, I knew it would come.'

Eyes fluttering closed, she nodded slowly.

'I tried, Eva. I tried to give you that fairy tale, without even realising what I was doing. Because I desired it too. From the start I was trying to make you mine. Tempting you with what I *could* give you. An engagement ring from my heart. Making love to you with everything I am. All the while thinking: she's mine. Mine. She is finally mine. And tomorrow I will tell her she must marry me. But then...*Cristo*, Eva, as soon as I touch you I lose my mind and I realise this sounds ludicrous but in my heart you were already my wife. Is that not odd, *cara*?'

Crushing her ruby-red lips, she shook her head wildly as if she understood.

'But neither of those things excuse the dishonour of not protecting you. I felt nothing but shame. Knew then I did not deserve to ask for your hand regardless. So yes, I pounced on the hope you were pregnant. Not for an heir, Eva. I pounced at the chance to have you.'

'I...I can't believe this is truly happening,' she said, breathless, pointed her unsteady hand at his chest. 'Did you just say "from the start"?'

'*Sì*,' he admitted. 'Looking back to Edward's vault, *Cristo*, I was consumed with the need to slip my ring upon your finger. Every word I said to you that day was truth. Every touch, every flower, every kiss, all from my heart.'

Another tear trickled down her face as she began to fidget in her seat. Moved to cross her legs into a yoga pose, as if she were trying to close the gap between them.

'Tell me something,' she said in a rush, her eyes darting over his face. 'When was the first time you saw me?'

In a second he was back in the cave. He'd known she wanted to ask him but he'd been too scared to lay his heart on the line. 'The night before we were introduced in the gardens, Finn and I arrived late from a club. I couldn't sleep. So I went down to the kitchen for water and there you were. Tousled. All lush hair and sexy long legs, wearing those skimpy shorts and vest tops you prefer. Looking for something to satisfy your sweet tooth, *cara*.'

'You watched me?' she asked with a pleasurable kind of wonder and he knew it was wrong, knew it was pointless, but his heart kicked with a hopeful beat.

'Oh, I watched you, Eva,' he murmured, voice thick and raspy. 'Do you want to know what I thought?'

'Yes,' she said quickly. 'Tell me.'

'I thought…' His voice cracked. So he swallowed. Tried again. 'She is an angel. I know I am not worthy of her and I know she could never love me, but I would move heaven and earth to make her mine.'

'You did?' she whispered, a beautiful watery smile touching her lips.

'I did. But that night in the pool-house, you were grieving, it was wrong to touch you. And then you asked me for only one night. One night would never have been enough for me, Eva. One million nights would never be enough.'

Her delicate hand fluttered to cover her heart and he watched her eyes fill with fresh tears and sorrow, her head bow. So much sadness and despair— neither good things, he knew—and that tentative bud of hope withered and died inside his chest.

Dante slid forward on the hard wood, closer to the edge, closer to her. 'I am leaving but I need you to know this, Eva. The true reason I am telling you all of this.'

Snap went his control and he picked up her warm hand, wrapped it in one of his, squeezing tight. Then he tucked his forefinger under her chin, lifting her head to lock with her eyes for the last time.

Cupping her jaw, he smoothed over her cheek with the pad of his thumb. One last time. 'I know you can never return my heart but if you *ever* need me, I am here for you. Only one phone call away. I swear you would always come first. I vow I would take care of you on the darkest of days and never let you fall. Promise me you will remember that.'

'Oh, Dante.'

'Swear it to me, Eva!'

'I…I promise,' she said, tears now falling in earnest. Tears he caught, wiped away with his thumb. Tears that broke his heart.

'*Cara*, do not cry, *per favore*. I cannot bear it. I will leave.' He had her oath. It would have to be enough.

Dante stood, still bent at the waist, and leaned forward to touch her brow with his lips. Every agonised bone in his body screamed and a strange sensation stung the backs of his eyes as he spoke against her soft skin, 'I will always love you, Eva.'

Then he pulled back, to stand, to turn, to walk away…

'No!' Eva reached up, cupped his gorgeous, if a little bewildered, face, sank her fingers into his thick yummy hair and tugged his mouth down to hers. 'Don't leave me again. I need you.'

Then she kissed him, kissed him, kissed him until he *finally* kissed her back.

True, it wasn't the most passionate kiss they'd ever shared—it was messy, dewy from her tears and there were too many emotions cluttering it up, but it was stupendously wonderful. Especially when Dante snapped out of his stupor, gripped her waist and lifted her from the sofa as he stood tall, crushing her to him, lashing the strength of his steely arms around her. Making her feel precious. His most prized possession. *Oh*, how she'd missed him. Craved him night and day.

Desperate hands touched everywhere they could reach, wild sounds of need filled the air around them and it was love. So much love. Yet the man had no idea of the love swelling her heart. Only for him.

Dante tore his mouth free. 'Eva…*cara mia*?' he said, just as breathless as her, his wide chest heaving. 'What *exactly* does this mean?'

'Oh, Dante.' Brushing a thick lock of hair from his brow, she sank into his deep, dark, tortured gaze. 'It means I love you. I always have. It was love, obsession and lust at first glance. Within ten minutes, I'd designed my wedding gown and picked out stationery and china.'

Face contorting, he shook his head, adamant. 'No. You have not always…loved me. You asked me for one night, Eva. One night.'

'Because I thought that was all you would give me. And I wanted my first time to be with you. Only you.' She remembered then, his exact words. Now imprinted on her brain. *One million nights would never be enough*. He loved her. He truly loved her. She was still having trouble believing this wasn't some pheromone-induced hallucination and from the look of it she wasn't the only one.

'*Cristo*,' he said, rocking back on his heels. And, before she knew it, he plunged down to the coffee table.

'I can't believe you didn't see it.'

'I had no idea,' he said, lifting his head. 'I thought, for you, it was just sexual attraction, passion. I didn't think love was possible for me.'

Eva blinked. 'Says the man with a jar of tattered hearts.'

'Hearts longing for my money, Eva. You ask my ex-wife why she agreed to my father's lucrative proposal. Only to sleep with my half-brother Lazio weeks later. I found them together.'

Eva slumped back down onto the sofa opposite. 'No wonder you were so cynical about women. I wish you'd told me.'

'In the seven weeks we were married I think I saw her two, three times. I sabotaged her every effort, Eva. Without really understanding why. When I found them entwined I felt nothing but anger at myself and sheer relief. Natalia said she couldn't compete with Vitale but it isn't until now I realise she was competing with you.'

'Oh, Dante.'

'I do not blame her any more. If she feels for Lazio one hundredth of what I feel for you, I understand perfectly.'

'Why didn't you tell me how you felt all those years ago?'

Raking his hand around the back of his neck, he exhaled a long ragged breath. 'My mother used to tell me I was like my father. Cold. Dark. Unlovable. But since you and I talked I was beginning to think she was beyond sad. Demoralised. I think he did that to her. And I reminded her of him every single day.'

Eva stroked down the side of his face with the back of her fingers. 'You're not cold, Dante. You're white-hot heat. And yes, you're dark, but I love you for it. It draws me in and it turns me on.' Just talking about his dark male dominance sent ribbons of heat through her veins.

Licking her suddenly dry lips, she told him, 'I crave you. All that dark smouldering passion makes me feel alive. But you have this other side too. It's always been there. Like when you held my hand the day of my mother's funeral. It's your secret side. It's Dream Falls. It's the man who showed me not to be afraid of my body. It's the man who came in here and opened his heart, expecting nothing in return. Only wishing to be there for me. It's the man I'm proud of, the man who is more worthy than any other I know. The most lovable man in the world.'

'Eva?' he said, as if doubting, trying to believe, as he swooped down for another kiss, this one no less desperate than the last.

Down, down they went, tumbling onto the sofa, his hard weight pressing her into the plush cushions. And Eva thrust her fingers in his thick hair and held on tight as he spent all his doubt, all his fears, all his anguish by making love with sliding lips, his tongue slow and easy, stirring her insides with seductive persuasion.

'Eva...Eva...tell me again, *cara*.'

'I love you,' she said on a panting breath. 'Always.'

Closing his eyes for a beat, he delved into the inside pocket of his dark suit. Pulled out his fist. Unfurled his fingers.

'Oh, Dante,' she cried, her eyes filling, spilling over, tears trickling down her face.

'*Cristo*, Eva, these are good tears, *Sì?*'

'Yes,' she said, 'yes,' dashing them away. 'But how *could* you toss it into the lake? I was furious with you.'

Contrition slashed across his high cheekbones. 'Not my finest moment, *cara*. I thought I'd lost you for ever. I went back the moment you left the island. I swear it.' He slipped her beautiful yellow diamond down her ring finger, embedding the heavy weight, and everything fell right in the world.

'So many people have let you down in your life and then I did the same. But I was so scared that day. I didn't want to need your love. The only control I had was to be the one who left. Before I sank even deeper.'

Dante caught her wrist and pulled her hand down to press flat over his heart, the accelerating beat echoing her own. 'Marry me, Eva. Let me make you mine. No contracts. No baby if you wish. Just you and me.'

Fresh tears stung the backs of her eyes. How many times had she dreamed of this moment? Just like this. With pure, unadulterated love in his eyes.

Then it struck her. What he'd said.

'Hold on. No baby if I wish? But I might be already.'

'What?' He reared back a touch. 'You said you were not.'

'No, I said I didn't know yet. I've been working up the courage to do the test. Praying I was because I wanted your baby so much and I've been so miserable without you. I was half-tempted to sign your stupid contract. The pain when you're not close…'

'Ah, Eva,' he said, nuzzling deliciously down her jaw, pressing his lips to her neck. 'I feel it too, *cara.*'

'Then I felt selfish for wanting your love when it may only bring you pain. Except…'

He sucked gently on the pulse throbbing at the base of her throat. 'It is worse without one another.'

'Yes,' she said, curling her face into him, breathing in his dark, rich scent, heat spiralling down her midriff. 'Now we can do the test together, right?'

'Later.' Lips curving in that devilish half smile that made her tummy flip, he launched to his feet and *whoosh* she was in his arms and his lips were crashing over hers once more, his tongue a velvet lash of tormenting pleasure.

Body coiling with sweet anticipation, she wrapped her legs tight around his waist, gyrating against the thick length of his ardour, revelling in the growl rumbling up his chest as he made his way through to her bedroom.

'I have work to do.' He tossed her atop the bed and tore his jacket from his shoulders.

Writhing against the pearly-pink coverlet, she watched him tear off his shirt, gingerly snap his trousers open over what she guessed was a whole load of hard, pained want. Only for her. 'You still haven't given me your answer.'

Eva smiled. Rose to her knees and inched the hem of her dress up and over her head. 'Oh, so we're talking proposals here?'

Dante kicked his trousers to the floor, his gaze enraptured, burning through her white lacy knickers, his words tight. 'We certainly are. I have developed a penchant for persuading you. Teasing, tempting.'

Eva flipped the front catch of her bra and sank back against the cushions, her legs scissoring with impatience. 'Go ahead, do your worst, Vitale.'

'Fear not, *cara*,' he growled, crawling over her, all raw predator grace. 'I intend to...'

A long while later...

Sprawled on crumpled sheets, facing one another, Dante entwined his legs with hers and corkscrewed a lock of her hair around his finger, languishing in contentment, a happiness he'd never known before. 'So which of the screaming yeses was agreeing to marry me, *cara mia*?'

'All fifty of them. Your technique is astoundingly good.'

No. It was all her. Only Eva could make him feel

this insatiable. Invincible. Worthy. And watching her glorious body tense in exquisite violence when she came in the throes of ecstasy was downright addictive.

'I aim to please,' he murmured, cupping her breast in his palm, luxuriating in the way she pushed into his hand. 'Although I would like to hear it one last time before that little stick turns blue.'

'Even you can't make me come in ninety seconds, Dante.'

'Wanna bet?' he growled, cinching her waist and rolling onto his back, taking Eva with him.

A purely feminine laugh stretched her lips wide as she straddled him and tugged the covers over their heads. 'I love you,' she breathed, undulating to take him inside her.

White heat unfurled high on each of his thighs and while he could still speak he said huskily, 'I love you too, *cuore mio*. Always.'

Dante gripped the delicious curves of her behind, groaning when she wrenched her lips free and leaned towards the night stand. Still he kept hold, so she never left the tight lock of his body.

'It's midnight.' White stick in hand, she came back and whispered against his lips. 'Merry Christmas, my darling.'

Heart hammering against his ribcage, he could scarcely breathe. What he'd done to deserve such a gift as Eva, he'd never know. But as he snaked his hands up her waist to wrap his arms around her, he knew he was never letting her go.

'After three we both look,' she said. 'One, two, three…'

Dante didn't look at the stick. He didn't need to. The answer was written all over her beautiful face. And right then he swore to do everything in his power to preserve that look of unadulterated joy, nourish it for the rest of their lives. Making every precious moment count.

* * * * *

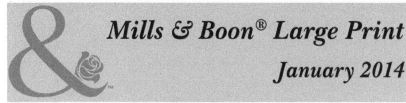

Mills & Boon® Large Print
January 2014

CHALLENGING DANTE
Lynne Graham

CAPTIVATED BY HER INNOCENCE
Kim Lawrence

LOST TO THE DESERT WARRIOR
Sarah Morgan

HIS UNEXPECTED LEGACY
Chantelle Shaw

NEVER SAY NO TO A CAFFARELLI
Melanie Milburne

HIS RING IS NOT ENOUGH
Maisey Yates

A REPUTATION TO UPHOLD
Victoria Parker

BOUND BY A BABY
Kate Hardy

IN THE LINE OF DUTY
Ami Weaver

PATCHWORK FAMILY IN THE OUTBACK
Soraya Lane

THE REBOUND GUY
Fiona Harper

Mills & Boon® Large Print
February 2014

THE GREEK'S MARRIAGE BARGAIN
Sharon Kendrick

AN ENTICING DEBT TO PAY
Annie West

THE PLAYBOY OF PUERTO BANÚS
Carol Marinelli

MARRIAGE MADE OF SECRETS
Maya Blake

NEVER UNDERESTIMATE A CAFFARELLI
Melanie Milburne

THE DIVORCE PARTY
Jennifer Hayward

A HINT OF SCANDAL
Tara Pammi

SINGLE DAD'S CHRISTMAS MIRACLE
Susan Meier

SNOWBOUND WITH THE SOLDIER
Jennifer Faye

THE REDEMPTION OF RICO D'ANGELO
Michelle Douglas

BLAME IT ON THE CHAMPAGNE
Nina Harrington

0114 Rom LP